Changeling Press LLC

ChangelingPress.com

Dragon's Egg
LGBTQ+ Dark Fantasy Romance
Lena Austin

Dragon's Egg
LGBTQ+ Dark Fantasy Romance
Lena Austin

ISBN: 978-1-60521-946-2

Publisher:
Changeling Press LLC
315 N. Centre St.
Martinsburg, WV 25404
ChangelingPress.com

Printed in the U.S.A.

Editor: Katriena Knights
Cover Artist: Angela Knight

The individual stories in this anthology have been previously released in E-Book format.

Table of Contents

Dragon's Egg
LGBTQ+ Dark Fantasy Romance
Lena Austin

In his nightmares, Jack's the kid from a children's song. But then dreams turn erotic as he makes love with the dragon in its human form.

When his therapist suggests he go back to Wales to find the cavern from his dreams, Jack resists. Then one last erotic dream proves the dragon is real, and he's dying. Now it's a race to save the Magic Dragon and discover Jack's past.

Chapter One

Jack Draper locked his hands behind his head and leaned back in his chair for a few minutes of much needed rest. He hadn't been sleeping well lately -- worse than usual. Lack of enough hours in the day was common enough when you owned a real estate empire, but the past few months he'd been lucky to get three or four hours. His therapist had finally given up after the best drugs on the planet couldn't knock him out cold without getting into dangerous dosages.

Speaking of which, he had an appointment with a specialist. He glanced at his watch. Fortunately, he owned this building, and the specialist's office was on the third floor, just a short trip down his private elevator.

Jack chuckled to himself. Private elevators, penthouse suites on the top floor of a luxury office complex in Manassas, Virginia, just outside Washington, DC, were not bad for an abandoned orphan from South Wales. Getting a scholarship to an American college had been his smartest move. Now, at age thirty-five, he was on top of the world. Literally.

He buzzed his secretary. "Janine, I've got an appointment. Usual orders."

Her crisp voice answered immediately. "Yes, sir. Don't forget your meeting with the Board of Directors at three, Mr. Draper."

He grumbled for a moment. "Yeah, I remember. Feed me lots of coffee, as usual, or I'll go to sleep on them." What a waste of time. He couldn't sleep at night, but those old walruses on the BOD could put him to sleep in fifteen minutes, nit-picking over every detail just to justify their expensive salaries and perks.

Jack grabbed up his briefcase and left his suit jacket hanging in the closet. He'd be damned if he'd dress up just to go lay on some shrink's couch. He had his cell and his Treo in the briefcase. That would do, if some emergency came up in the next two hours.

Dr. Lledrith was waiting for him in her office when her receptionist ushered him in. A formidable older woman with stone gray hair and a long nose, she stood and shook his hand in a firm grip. "Welcome, Mr. Draper."

Jack started. Her accent was as familiar as his own. "You're Welsh."

She assessed him with a cool eye. "Yes, I am. So are you, according to the file Dr. Bernstein sent. I understand you have few memories of your childhood."

Jack nodded and sat in the chair opposite her desk. "Correct. While I'm sure Dr. Bernstein provided you with his opinions, I'll say I can't agree with his theory that my childhood was so bad I've blocked the memory of it. It doesn't feel right to me."

She flipped through his file. "I tend to agree with you, Mr. Draper. What information I was able to gather beyond what Dr. Bernstein provided indicates a happy, well-rounded time until you left for college. It was in college that you began to have difficulties and showed antisocial patterns."

Jack bristled. "If you're referring to my being gay, I don't consider that antisocial."

Her thin lips quirked into a half-smile. "No, Mr. Draper. I'm referring to your wild behavior and disciplinary issues from your college record. Your homosexuality appears to be one of your few stabilities. You took some time to reconcile your sexuality, but that appears settled."

He subsided. Like so many gay men, he tended to be touchy about being homosexual in such a conservative town as Washington. "Sorry. It's a sore spot."

Dr. Lledrith gave him her first genuine smile, and it softened her whole face. "My apologies as well, Mr. Draper. I should have been specific. Your reputation for no nonsense conciseness is well known." She settled in her chair once more. "I believe your insomnia may stem from some event at college age, or perhaps just before you came to the US. How much do you remember of that time period?"

He shifted uncomfortably in the chair and longed for a cup of coffee. "Not much. That appears to be the blankest area in my memories. A space of about three months doesn't exist."

She steepled her fingers in front of her mouth, but the warm smile didn't fade. "I think we can work on that memory loss later. What concerns me presently is the insomnia. Tell me about it."

Jack sighed and suppressed a shudder. "It isn't truly insomnia where I can't sleep, but rather recurring dreams that awaken me after only a few hours." He paused, slightly uncomfortable. "Erotic dreams, at the end, though they start innocently enough."

Dr. Lledrith got up and poured them both a generous mug of coffee. She cocked an eyebrow at him as if to ask how he preferred to embellish his.

Jack shook his head and reached for the brew that had recently become his lifeline, despite what it was doing to the lining of his stomach.

Dr. Lledrith took her time adding a generous amount of creamer, and a generous dollop of what appeared to be honey. She returned to her seat, seemingly at ease. "Mr. Draper, I've been a therapist for quite a long time, and one of my sons is gay. I doubt seriously you could shock me. However, in the interests of your privacy, I shall not record the dream in any way. My memory will have to suffice. Does that ease your mind?"

"It does." Jack relaxed. He'd always been a man of great privacy. He hated the fetish pervading society to record every detail of life for posterity in online journals and websites.

The doctor sipped her coffee placidly, and even sniffed the aroma rising from the cup. "Glad to hear it. Please begin."

He drew breath, knowing it wasn't going to be easy to tell what he saw every night. Somehow, he trusted Dr. Lledrith much more than he'd trusted Dr. Bernstein. Perhaps it was hearing her accent. "Very well. As I said, the dream starts innocently. I'm a child. I'd say about ten years old. I'm playing on the cliffs not far from the orphanage where I grew up in South Wales. It must be a holiday, because I was diligent in my schoolwork and rarely went out when I had homework."

Dr. Lledrith nodded. "Yes, your grades were exemplary. All right, we'll assume it was either a weekend or a holiday."

Jack closed his eyes and couldn't help the smile that chased across his face. "We weren't supposed to play on the cliffs, of course, but I seemed to know the way down the rocks well. It may have been my only rebellion to play where I wasn't supposed to go."

Her voice softened, and was not intrusive. "You played alone, then?"

"Quite alone. I get the impression from my feelings that it suited me to escape to this place." He frowned for a moment. "I'd never been sociable, and always felt like the outsider."

She hmphed. He heard her flip papers. "Understandable. You were placed in the orphanage after having been found wandering the streets for apparently days. You wouldn't speak for weeks. The director named you Jack Draper because she constantly found you hiding behind the drapes and staring out the window."

Jack's eyes flew open. He turned and stared with his mouth agape. "I didn't know that. I'd always wondered."

Dr. Lledrith raised an eyebrow. "And you never thought to ask, even after you became an adult?"

Jack writhed in his chair. "I preferred to forget those years and erase my past, thank you. I'd always assumed my parents didn't want me and tossed me away like a bit of rubbish." His voice grew steely. "If they didn't love me enough to keep track of me, then I'd make my own way in the world and damn them."

Her eyes shut for a moment, then opened to give him a sympathetic smile. "While your achievements are admirable, Mr. Draper, I think your past may provide the key to your present difficulties. Please continue."

Jack got up to pace around the generous office. "Here I must admit to a bit of embarrassment. I believe my ego supplied an answer to my childish needs to feel important." He paused to admire the collection of books in the bookcase. "I supposed you've heard that children's song by Peter, Paul, and Mary?"

Dr. Lledrith chuckled. "You refer to 'Puff the Magic Dragon,' I believe. It's a natural leap for a child whose name is similar to the boy in the song to place himself in the story."

Jack winced as she hummed a few bars. "That's the one." He frowned and went back to sit down. He needed that cup of coffee like a man in the desert craved water. "I hate that song, strangely enough. I always have. The kid was a first class selfish heel. You don't desert your friends just because you grow up."

Dr. Lledrith's face was hidden by her coffee mug, but her shoulders stiffened. "Indeed they don't, if they're an honorable person, Mr. Draper. Usually, there's another unstated reason. Please continue with your dream. I assume there's a dragon in it."

Jack sucked in air gratefully. At least this therapist didn't consider him a nut and insist on analyzing the tiniest details of why his ego had superimposed his own face on that ridiculous song. "All right then. Yes, there's a cavern at the base of the cliffs. You have to step on a certain rock to see the entrance." He shrugged. "Magic, I suppose you'd call it in a child's lexicon."

She didn't bat an eyelash, much less smile. "Indeed. Go on."

He had to admire the lady's cool. "I have to jump a couple of spaces between boulders, but it's not that hard for an agile child. Once inside the entrance, the cave looks absurdly normal. Lichen, wet smooth walls from the water's action, the usual. I keep going into the dark interior, but the light behind me is enough to see by." He paused. "There's a dim light up ahead, too."

"Naturally. A child would need a light to see by to find his way." She got up and poured them both more coffee.

Jack was awed. "You're taking this all in stride. Dr. Bernstein had me analyzing every small illogical detail."

Dr. Lledrith raised one snowy eyebrow. "I'm not Dr. Bernstein. This is from the view of a child's mind. Therefore, things don't have to make logical sense.

They simply are. Children are so accepting, and don't question details. They might question why the sky is blue, but they don't need the science of it. Most of us should emulate the pure acceptance of a child."

"Thank you. I got rather exasperated by the nit picking. The child in me accepted it as right and proper." Jack shrugged. "Shall I continue?"

"Please do." She went back to placidly sipping her coffee, leaning comfortably back in her chair.

Jack gulped down his coffee despite the searing his tongue got. He needed the fortification. "As you might expect, yes, there was a dragon in the back cavern down a tunnel." He shut his eyes to better remember and relate. "An absolutely magnificent beast of purple and gold. Purple body, gold accents, I should say. His scales were iridescent, and glowed in the light. By the way, the light came from crystals embedded in the walls and ceiling of the cavern. Like a bloody rainbow."

"Sounds magnificent indeed. You should write, Mr. Draper. You have a way with words." Dr. Lledrith leaned forward and put her elbows on the desk. "You don't sound at all frightened of the dragon. Didn't you think he might like a snack of small boy?"

Jack laughed. "No, indeed! He was my friend, Puff."

"Puff is a child's name for something."

Jack nodded at her prompting. "I even supplied an answer for that, Dr. Lledrith. Puff had told me I couldn't pronounce his real name, so I'd been permitted to give him a name I could speak easily. I named him Puff because his nostrils would occasionally breathe a bit of smoke. I assume as an adult this means he was a fire-breathing dragon."

Again, Dr. Lledrith raised an eyebrow. "Is there any other kind?"

Jack laughed, even though he recognized the ploy to get him to talk about his personal obsession. "I find the subject of mythical creatures interesting, as you well know, Doctor. I have a hobby of cryptozoology, when I can afford the time to indulge." He grinned and winked. "When we are not on the clock, I can discourse about dragonkind for well over two hours without my notes, and present a full day's seminar with them."

She spread her fingers in a conciliatory gesture. "Caught me. Dr. Bernstein did mention your hobby, but not any expertise you might have. I can see his notes have as many holes in them as your memory."

Jack tossed an errant curl out of his eyes. He needed a haircut again. "Dr. Bernstein wasn't interested in my last trip to Puerto Rico, where I participated in a study of *chupacabre* predations. For some reason he considered it macabre."

Dr. Lledrith's voice was sardonic. "Most people would consider looking at eviscerated and bloodless corpses of farm animals to be so."

Jack's mouth fell open. "Very good, Doctor. Most people ask me what a *chupacabre* is, much less know what the evidence of their predations look like."

She shrugged. "So I watch intelligent telly upon occasion. Let's get back to your dream, please."

Jack tensed. "There's not much more to tell of the innocent portion, really. I hug Puff's neck and tell him how much I missed him, as if I've been away for a long time." He swallowed hard. "Then the dream changes."

* * *

Jack shifted in his chair and crossed his legs to hide the erection that was sure to appear. "I'll admit it's difficult to discuss this."

Dr. Lledrith gave him a sympathetic glance, and then turned her chair around so he couldn't see her at all. "Is this better?"

He stared at the back of her butter-colored leather chair. Not one gray hair showed over the top. What the hell -- it might work to pretend she didn't exist. "I'm willing to have a go." He winced at his word choice.

She didn't speak, but one hand rose into view and waved languidly at him to continue. The implication was that she'd not speak or ask questions, merely absorb.

Jack sipped from his cooling coffee and glanced at his watch. Not much time remained before his PDA would beep, reminding him of his hated meeting.

"I'm hugging Puff's neck and I change. I'm now grown to late adolescence, I'd say. I'm taller, anyway, and I've a host of body aches I remember afflicted me then."

Her chair creaked as she changed position, but she still didn't speak.

Jack took that as a sign to continue. "Puff changes too. Instead of a dragon, I'm now holding and being held by a man. A finely formed one, with black hair. Only the eyes remain the same to let me know it's still Puff. Golden brown eyes like the finest whiskey." Jack drew a ragged breath. "We're both naked, suddenly."

No movement, no sound from Dr. Lledrith.

"I'm the one who initiates the kiss. I want that clear. This isn't some superimposed child sexual abuse. I want him as badly as he appears to want me."

Jack closed his eyes and struggled to remember. "This part is in bits and pieces. Very foggy. I have papers in my hand. One of them is my college acceptance letter. I recognize the letterhead when I break the kiss and look down for a moment.

"Then, I just don't care. Puff is leading me to the big stone he used as a dragon couch. It's got a hollow in the center, I suppose where his dragon body has rubbed a depression in the sandstone."

Dr. Lledrith's hand appeared, holding her coffee cup. He assumed she let him see it just to show him she still was listening.

He let out the breath he'd held. Her trick of "disappearing" from view was working. It was easier to say the words.

"Puff tugs on my hand, and I go willingly back into his arms. Part of me is shocked at my behavior, and part of me revels in it. I've never felt so alive as I do in this dream.

"Puff pulls us both into the center of his couch. It's clean and warm there, as if it has been freshly scrubbed just for the occasion. He lands on his back at the bottom, and just lays there."

A minute creak of the doctor's chair allowed Jack to assume she listened.

"'I won't force you, Jackie,' Puff says. 'You're in charge of this. When you say stop, we stop. I'll not have it said I seduced a boy.'

"I'm stung by this. I tell him, 'I'm eighteen, and I know my own mind. I love you, Puff, and this is the only way I have to prove it.' He might say something then, but I'm fierce and attack his... his..." Jack stopped and blushed, unwilling to use the usual word in his vocabulary.

Dr. Lledrith's voice floated softly over the back of the chair. "I believe the word is cock, isn't it, in the common vernacular? Or would you prefer to use something more crude or clinical?"

Jack choked for a moment. "Er, cock will do I think. Um, there are quite a few terms I could use."

"Then stop being squeamish, Mr. Draper. I assure you, I know what one looks, tastes, and feels like, though not from your perspective of course."

The inference was clear. She knew he was gay, but this was more intimate than anything he'd discussed with Dr. Bernstein. "Er, no, I suppose you do."

She didn't turn around, but he could hear the rich good humor in her voice. "Consider this, Mr. Draper. You and I both like the same things. I happen to be quite fond of fellatio, myself."

Jack started. He'd never considered that aspect of having a female therapist. They did have the same tastes in common when it came to sexual partners. "Well, I won't ask you if you enjoy flavored lotions or not, but that does put a new perspective on it."

"Like most females, I'm inordinately fond of chocolate sauce. Please continue, Mr. Draper."

"I didn't need to know that. Yes, ma'am. Yes, I perform fellatio on Puff." Jack swallowed another sip of cold coffee. "Er, suffice it to say I enjoy myself?"

"Only if you did," she replied briskly. "I do hope he returns the favor?"

Jack prevented himself from spattering his mouthful of coffee all over her elegant desk and his file scattered atop it. He blushed and was grateful she couldn't see him. "Er, well, yes."

"Excellent. Reciprocity indicates a feeling of equality. I'm pleased so far, and --"

Simultaneously, his PDA and her electronic timer on her desk beeped, ending their session.

Regretfully, Jack rose to his feet and hid his rock hard and aching erection with his briefcase.

The doctor turned her chair around. "We've begun very well, Mr. Draper. I'm pleased. Tonight, should you dream again, please try to remember details. I'd like to see you again, first thing in the morning. I shall be here as early as seven, if you wish." She offered her hand. "I have a theory formulating. Let me think on it, and I may have a simple but effective therapy we may try."

Jack shook her hand and fled. Sleep was now the last thing on his mind. Were it not for that damned board meeting, he'd be down at the local spa to find someone to ease the ache in his cock.

Jack slugged down the last of the warm milk his secretary had suggested that afternoon and crawled wearily into his bed. When not even the finest Egyptian cotton sheets and the most expensive mattress guaranteed a restful night, he doubted sixteen ounces of heated moo juice would improve things. Part of him hoped he'd dream again, and part of him prayed he didn't. "Something's got to give, and soon, or I'll be a candidate for the local Bedlam."

Not surprisingly, he tossed and turned, unable to get comfortable. He considered flipping on the television, but decided he didn't need to get angry over the real estate charlatans populating the late night channels, hawking incomplete information on how to get involved in foreclosures.

Jack grumbled and punched his pillow into a more comfortable shape. To the empty air and all those people who might be taken in by that scam, he muttered, "Reality check, people. If you could afford all the costs associated with buying and renovating, you'd be doing it on your own home. I ought to write a book myself."

His eyes flew open. That wasn't such a bad idea. He'd made a success of honest real estate entrepreneurship. Maybe he *should* write a book. He scribbled a few notes on his bedside tablet without bothering with the lamp.

Satisfied, he grinned and flopped back into the pillows. He fell asleep in the middle of outlining chapters in his head.

Chapter Two

Jack climbed over the rocks, clutching his precious letters. Joyously, he stamped extra hard on the flat granite rock that allowed him to see the cavern opening.

His worn trainers made no sound on the rocks, and only a slight whisper on the sand at the entrance to the dragon cave. He knew the way blindfolded to the back chambers, where he knew his dragon rested in the early morning hours.

"Puff! Puff! I've wonderful news!" His teenaged self skidded to a halt just inside the back entrance.

The great dragon opened his eyes and raised his head. "Indeed, Jackie? Well, come in and we'll have tea. You've been very busy of late, haven't you?"

Jackie strutted in, now assured of his welcome. "I'd love some tea, thanks."

Puff changed into a human man, dressed in medieval clothing that would have made a cat laugh under normal circumstances. His fine brocade gambeson, long dark hair, and leather trews fit his personality, but were woefully out of fashion. He strode over to a table and fireplace and filled a kettle from a small waterfall that fell into a stone basin. "Shall I heat it with my breath, or make do with the fireplace?"

Jackie walked over and laid his letter on the table near his accustomed place. "The fireplace, if you please. I'm not starving." For the first time, he felt a frisson of nerves. "I'd like to talk with you as a man, if you don't mind."

The dragon-man sighed with mock disappointment. "No flying today? What a shame." He knelt at the hearth and blew gently, starting a small fire with the wood Jackie brought him on a regular basis from his wandering in the forest.

Jackie guiltily noted the supply was low. "Sorry I've not been around to bring you fuel for your fire, Puff."

The kettle swung into place. Puff didn't turn around. "I've managed, Jackie. I knew you'd be busy until the summer holidays with school." He turned around and laughed. "If nothing else, I'll burn this old table. Then, the next time you visit you'll have to eat your meal on my couch."

Jackie eyed the great stone slab where the dragon's body slept. "That wouldn't be very comfortable. I'd imagine it's cold and hard."

Puff laughed and placed a bowl of fruit on the table. "Nonsense. I keep it quite warm. As you can imagine, I feel the cold much more than you humans do."

Jackie nodded. "Of course. I studied that in school. You're a reptile, and cold-blooded. I don't see how you keep warm in winter, though." The last had to be shouted over the whistle of the teakettle.

Puff presented him with a cup of tea and took one for himself. They sat in their chairs, sipping from the delicious brew. "I use my breath to warm my couch. I have to be careful, though. Too much, and I'll not have enough of the special air in my body I use to fly. Makes it difficult to hunt over the sea that way." He saluted Jackie with his mug. "Did that once as a hatchling, and had to swim for my dinner. The cold of the sea made it very uncomfortable until I found a nice large school of fish. I was certain I'd freeze to death. Haven't repeated that mistake again."

Jackie put his chin in his hands. "Is that how you make the special flying air? Eating fish?"

Puff shrugged. "Well, I think so. When I don't eat, I don't fly. That's all I care to know. But I doubt you came here to find out how dragons fly."

Jackie picked at the corner of his letter. "No, but someday I do want to know how you make magic as well."

Puff's golden eyes turned stern and cool. "That's a dragon secret. Ask me again in a few years. I might tell you then. What's the paper?"

Jackie sighed for a moment, and hid his disappointment. "Next week, next year, ten years. Bloody hell, Puff. I'm eighteen as of last week, so they say."

Puff sipped his tea, completely unruffled. "That's merely the day the orphanage gave you to celebrate. We'll wait and be sure. One extra turn of the sun won't kill you. Now, what's the paper? I won't ask again."

In the mercurial way the young had, Jackie's face cleared. He picked up the paper and waved it. "I've been accepted into the American college! I shall have a full scholarship! An American church will sponsor me for everything the college doesn't provide. This is my college acceptance letter."

Puff rose stiffly from his chair and poured himself more tea. "So, you'll be leaving for America soon? When?"

The sadness in his voice made Jackie want to run and do something so unmanly as to hug him. He squelched it. He'd prove he was a man. "In a few weeks. Puff, this is my dream come true! I've worked so hard, hoping some college would overlook my humble state and give me a chance."

Jackie slammed back the chair and stood, suddenly in a rage at the hand the fates had dealt him. "I've always been 'that poor little orphan.' Well, I don't want to be him anymore. If my parents didn't love me enough to keep me, then I've got to fight for myself." His fist pounded the table for emphasis.

A large hand covered Jackie's.

Jackie looked up into his friend's golden eyes, so full of pain and secrets.

The dragon's words came softly on a sigh. "I love you, and I always have."

Jackie's anger melted away, but not his defiance. "Yeah, my dragon friend? Prove it." He bent across the table and kissed Puff.

* * *

Jack Draper sat up in bed, breathing hard. His clenched fist still rested on his own thigh, and the pain throbbed. He'd have a bruise in the morning from beating on his own flesh.

He scrubbed his face and glanced at the clock. Two o'clock in the morning. Five hours to go before he saw the doctor again. "Oh, geez. What does this mean? How in the bloody hell am I going to explain this?"

* * *

Dr. Lledrith sipped her coffee and pondered for what seemed like an eternity to Jack. The muted sounds of early morning traffic barely breached the silence of her office.

Jack fidgeted and wondered if he'd destroyed her theories and his chances of treatment. As long as the therapies she devised didn't involve needles or electricity, he was game.

"I think you should go to South Wales, Mr. Draper. In fact, as soon as possible." Dr. Lledrith's no-nonsense command broke Jack's reverie.

Jack shot from his chair. Fear tingled up his spine, but he channeled it into anger. "Just like that, Doc? I should simply forego all my business, cancel all my appointments, and fly to Wales? I thought I was the mental one here."

Dr. Lledrith held up a hand, though her smile never wavered. "The treatment is called aversion therapy, Mr. Draper. Simply put, it means the patient is exposed to situations or things that are related to their condition until the condition is reduced. For instance, a person who fears spiders might at first be exposed to pictures of arachnids until they no longer react with fear, then they are shown caged spiders, and finally they may actually hold a tarantula without fear. Aversion therapy is very effective in some cases."

Jack dismissed all this with a wave of his hand. He had visions of singing the song or having it sung to him for hours on end. "That's all well and good, Doctor, but what do you hope to accomplish with this trip for me? I don't fear anything."

Dr. Lledrith raised an eyebrow. "Then why are you sweating, Mr. Draper? My office is chilled to a balmy seventy-two degrees. Why do you awaken in the middle of the night from the simple imagery of making love with a man? Finally, why are there gaping holes in your memory your dragon could fly through? Ponder that, Mr. Draper."

Jack snarled inwardly, but kept a reasonably neutral expression on his face as best he could. He was proud of his newly acquired American citizenship and had no desire to return to Wales. Beside all the emotional reasons, he had business appointments scheduled until the end of next week and a recently acquired apartment building to renovate in Georgetown. He wasn't about to let anyone screw up the lovely nineteenth century architecture without his oversight of the plans. "I have too much to do for me to simply drop all my work and hare off for however long it might take to get me some sleep. I'd rather be knocked out with a sledgehammer."

Dr. Lledrith's eyes narrowed and the fingers of her right hand twitched, as if she longed to take notes. "Mr. Draper, I beg you to consider this option. The bags under your eyes resemble a luggage factory. You're pale, and judging from the way that tailored Armani suit hangs on you, you've lost a significant amount of weight. I'm very concerned about your health." She paused and flipped open her PDA. "I'll make a deal with you. I can be free of my own appointments in a few days. If you fly out by Monday, I could join you on Wednesday."

Jack snatched up his briefcase and strode toward the door, despite their having fifteen more minutes of appointment time left. Over his shoulder, he tossed out his briskest tone of voice that made most of his employees quail with fear. "Impossible. I couldn't possibly leave before Monday next without annoying many business contacts. However, I'll ask my secretary to free up a large block of time next month for a bit of skiing or something. A vacation does sound like a good idea." He was out the door and entered the waiting elevator as if demons chased him. His demon just happened to be a mythical creature from a children's song. "Never let it be said I have ordinary neuroses." The doors closed. He leaned against the wall of the elevator and laughed at himself.

* * *

Jack placed the brandy snifter on the coffee table with exaggerated care. The table wavered when his eyes unfocused. "Drinking yourself into unconsciousness is not smart, old boy."

He ran fingers through his hair and rubbed his aching head. "Neither is working yourself to exhaustion from before dawn until after dark."

The room swayed, and Jack lay back on the pillows of the monstrously large suede sofa he'd mockingly called his "napping sofa." The sofa easily accommodated his long frame when he didn't want to bother with his bed. Lately, the couch had seemed infinitely preferable.

He kicked off his shoes and threw his legs up on the sofa to stretch aching muscles. "God, I'm tired. A ski trip sounds like too much exercise. Perhaps I'll find a quiet beach and someone to serve me drinks under an umbrella instead."

Thoughts of the whoosh of the sea as the waves rushed to shore and the cries of gulls made him think of the cliffs of Wales. In the midst of chastising himself for memories or lack thereof, he fell asleep.

Instantly, he was back at the cave, standing barefoot in the clothes he'd worn that day, minus the tie and jacket he'd left on the back of his sofa. The sea spray spattered his Armani pants.

Jack shivered in the cold night air. "The subconscious mind has more ways of making me obey than I have ways of avoiding the message. Maybe the doctor is right. If I stop fighting the dreams, maybe some clue will appear as to why the visions haunt me. I might as well play along." Resigned to a short night, he stepped into the cavern and marched determinedly toward the back once more.

But this time, Puff barely raised his head. "Back again, are you? Well, flit about and be gone, you ghostly apparition. Leave me to die in peace, if you please."

The weak, tired voice was not the robust tones of old. The dragon's scales were dull and some gold and purple ones the size of dinner plates littered the ground around the stone bed.

The boy in Jack longed to run over and hug the dragon's neck. Who couldn't feel pity to see a dragon so bedraggled? "You look like hell, old man," Jack muttered.

"Oh, so now he speaks to me. I stand amazed. Okay, I lay amazed. What does a ghost want with a sick old dragon anyway? Answer me that." Puff shut his eyes, clearly not expecting an answer.

"Am I a ghost? I feel real to me." Jack looked down, and to his own eyes, he appeared as solid as the rock walls of the cavern. "In fact, it's cold in here. It's got to make your bones ache." In fact, he was positive a reptile as large as a dragon must be close to torpid and in severe pain, if Jack was shivering.

Puff's eyes remained shut. "Pain tells me I'm still alive, damn it. If you don't like the chill, you do something about warming the place up, then. And shut up. I'm trying to die in peace here."

Jack ground his teeth together and stormed back outside. "Irascible bastard. One breath, and he'd have a warm cave. No, he's got a martyr complex. He has to suffer before he dies. Idiot. Well, dammit, I'm cold and I don't feel like being a martyr."

He climbed the cliff wall, which seemed shorter than his memory supplied. He stomped into the woods at the top of the cliff and found a load of deadfall easily enough.

The climb down the cliffs in the tricky early morning light, carrying a huge pile of firewood, was more difficult than he cared to think about. His foot slipped on the wet rocks. He slid halfway down a boulder, straining and cursing at the scrape on his left anklebone.

Jack took a moment to examine the injury. The bleeding was minimal, but the whole ankle throbbed, warning him he'd probably twisted it a little. "Good thing this is a dream, or I'd be in trouble tomorrow," he snickered. He'd never felt any aftereffects from his dreams before, thank goodness.

Puff was still in the same position, and his sides moved indicating he breathed. The movement was the only sign of life.

Jack ignored the dragon just as Puff pretended to ignore him. He smiled to himself, and then threw the pile of sticks and small branches in the dusty fireplace. He pulled out a lighter attached to a Swiss Army knife he kept in his pocket for emergencies, and lit a few leaves. The fire flared to life.

The kettle sat in isolation nearby on the hearth. Jack blew off the dust and disturbed a spider's web. He filled the neglected iron kettle from the small waterfall and placed it on the hook to heat.

Proud and satisfied with himself, Jack turned and noticed the table and chairs were gone. So was the small cupboard where Puff had kept his teas and other human foods, if his dreams were accurate.

Jack put his hands on his hips, and for the first time since he'd returned, faced Puff fully. "Did you burn both the table set and the cupboard, Puff?"

"No, the cupboard is behind me, though it's a bit spare of…" The dragon's eyes flew open and he jumped as if his stone couch had become red hot. "Jackie? Are you my ghostly visitor? Is this why I'm dying? You're dead already?" He peered wildly at Jack, blinking.

Jack laughed to see the change in the great purple dragon. Something so big shouldn't be afraid of anything short of a nuclear bomb. "I'm not dead, you silly dragon. I'm dreaming in my home back in America."

The teakettle whistled sharply.

Jack shoved at Puff's tail until it moved and climbed behind him to find the cupboard, taking care not to put weight on his sore ankle. "Now change form and come have some tea, if you've any left."

Puff stared at his tail where Jack touched. "Feels real enough. All right then, I'll change. Maybe we're both dreaming."

The tail disappeared from Jack's path, so Jack crouched to rummage in the cupboard's contents. All he found was one red tin of tea and another of moldy biscuits. The teacups on their hooks were so filthy they'd have to be washed. He shook a beetle carcass out of one of the two he took from their hooks. "Geez, Puff, don't you ever clean anymore?"

Puff, now in his human form, snorted. "What was the point? It's been just me in here since you left." He stood with his arms crossed, as querulous as an old man. Nothing could hide his beauty, though he was thinner than Jack remembered. His cheeks were sunken, and the rings under his eyes were darker than Jack's.

Jack limped up to him and clapped him on the arm briefly. It was his dream, and they'd been lovers many times before in slumber. Why not act as if they were great friends now? "Well, I'm here now. We may as well enjoy our dream together."

Puff gasped in shock. "For a dream, you're solid enough. All right then, I can play along as well. Give me the tea. You've been in America far too long and you'd ruin the brewing."

Jack laughed and handed over the red tin. He washed the mugs in the stream of water and took off his shirt to use as a towel to dry them now that the cavern was warming up nicely.

Puff stumbled to the kettle, and sat at the hearth. His fumbling movements were not like the old Puff of Jack's dreams.

Jack frowned and walked over to put the cups on the hearth. Then, he got a good look at Puff's face. More specifically, his eyes. "Good God, Puff. No wonder you think I'm a ghost. You've got cataracts!"

Puff lifted his golden eyes, which now resembled an odd mix of whiskey and cream. "I do?" His voice sounded resigned to what Jack considered a serious death threat to a large predator like a dragon.

While his studies told him most reptilians were scent hunters, sight could not be ignored. It would be damn hard to hunt fish in the sea without the ability to see the shimmer of shoals of fish.

Jack took a moment to throw a larger log on the fire and control his emotions. He wanted to be angry, and he wanted to kiss a dragon. He really was insane. "I'd say you're damn near blind, old friend."

Chapter Three

Puff lowered his gaze and sat up ramrod straight. "I suppose it doesn't matter. I hunt fish by smell and hearing anyway, not by sight. Don't give it a second thought."

"Too late. I've already had lots of thoughts and discarded most of the options, like flying you to America in your human form and paying for the surgery." He waited until Puff finished snorting with laughter. "Yeah, I thought about the fact that, as soon as you were unconscious, you'd probably revert back to your natural form. That might be a bit disastrous."

Puff tossed back his black and silver hair. "To say the least."

Jack grabbed Puff's shirtfront. "Then it won't kill you to bend down here and let me have a closer look, will it?" The dragon remained stubbornly upright. He tugged harder.

Puff resisted every inch of the way, moving stiffly to bend down. "Am I allowed no pride?"

Jack studied the milky eyes as best he could in the dim light of the fire. "What's pride got to do with it? All I want is to have a look. Hold still." He lifted a hand to cup Puff's chin.

Puff jumped up and wobbled slightly from weakness. "Stop it, Jackie. It's not right."

Jack sat on the hearth, absorbing the dragon's wild mood swings. Then, it hit him. This Puff of his dreams was as gay as he was, and attracted to him. Jack stole a glance to Puff's pants. The tunic didn't hide the erection jutting through the fabric. "I see. My apologies, Puff. I didn't mean to tease."

Jack stood. He wanted Puff as much as the dragon wanted him, insanely enough. He cast about for a way to put Puff at ease. "The tea is undoubtedly ready. Are you warm enough?"

Puff raised a sardonic eyebrow, and his voice was heavy with irony. "Yes, I believe I am, if you refer to my body temperature." He squared his shoulders. "Yes, tea would be lovely."

Jack reached for the steaming kettle, but Puff batted his hand away. "You can't take the heat. Allow me."

Jack appreciated the double entendres flying back and forth between them. "I can so take the heat, but I'll allow you the privilege of being in charge, at least this time."

His drawled words had the desired effect. Puff shot him an unfocused look, and turned back to lift the hot kettle with his bare hands. He poured the tea into the cups with studious care. "So you say."

Jack picked up his cup and matched the dragon's ironic smile. "Indeed I do." He limped with deliberate steps to the dragon's stone pedestal and sat on the edge. He knew he now sat on Puff's bed wearing nothing but a pair of pants. He hoped the silent invitation was clear.

Puff gave Jack an opaque look. The only sound was the faint rush of the sea, the tinkle of the waterfall in the basin, and the hum between them that was purely mental. Puff's eyes narrowed. "Stop teasing, Jackie. It's not nice."

Knowing Puff could not possibly see facial expressions over the dimly lit distance between them, Jack snorted. "You seem to think I am. I'm not. Are you going to take me up on the invitation, or will you force me to be crude and blunt?"

One elegant silver and black eyebrow lifted toward Puff's hairline. "Yes. I want you to be crude and blunt. Tell me what you want, Jackie."

Jack sighed, making it deliberately loud. "Very well. One, could you manage to call me Jack? I've not been called Jackie since I left."

Puff sipped his tea. "I think I can manage that. Now that you're a fully grown man, can you manage my real name of Aneurin?"

Jack choked back laughter. "I can indeed, Aneurin. It fits you better, to call you the Welsh name for gold. Your golden eyes haunted my dreams for many a night."

The dragon put the cup down with deliberate care. "You've been dreaming of me?"

Jack took a sip of his tea, slurping deliberately. "Yes. Dreams of you and I making love, right here on this great bloody bed of yours."

Puff-Aneurin stared at the floor. "And you don't mind this dream?"

"At first, I minded. Only in that I didn't think it was right to be making love with a character from a children's song."

Puff chuckled. "Should have never gone to the pub and had a few pints. Told some idiot songster while I was in my cups, but retained enough sense to make it a tale." He shrugged. "Didn't expect the song to cross the pond."

"Puff, er, Aneurin... sorry. That song was sung in the 1960's before I was born." It had always bugged him that the song was older than he by nearly a decade.

"Oh. That. I went back in time to find some good ale, not that watered down piss they sell these days. I've heard in America they sell it cold, much to my horror." Aneurin grinned at his dig on Jack's adopted home.

Jack breathed a sigh of relief. Not only was Aneurin in a better mood, he actually looked like health and energy flowed back into him. "Not the same brews, you old-fashioned dragon. It's made to be served cold. Tastes horrid warm, I assure you."

"Oh. Well then. That's different. Are you going to finish telling me what you want? Or have you changed your mind?"

Jack gulped the rest of his tea, stood, and walked over to slap the empty cup beside Aneurin. He leaned forward until he was nose-to-nose with the man who'd haunted his dreams for months. "I want to drag you over to that stone couch, rip your clothes from your body, and start by tasting what lies beneath. What happens after that is by mutual consent, but I'm hoping you and I will both not sit well tomorrow. Is that clear enough?"

Aneurin's whiskey eyes grew round. He swallowed. "Clear as rain water."

Jack drew one hand up from Aneurin's chest, sliding a finger up his neck until he cupped Aneurin's chin. "I know I'm home, sleeping in my bed. I don't care if this is a dream. I'm planning on seeing this through until the end." His lips hovered above Aneurin's. "Half of me hopes this isn't a dream, and that you're healthy enough for a little exercise."

Aneurin leaned into his lips, making the lightest of contact. "I think we're both dreaming, but it's the happiest dream I've had since you left. The joy alone gives me the strength to go on."

Jack closed his eyes to savor the soft brush of their lips. "You talk too much, dragon. Kiss me, and we'll pretend this isn't a dream."

"You've gotten pushy since you grew up. I like it." Aneurin leaned further, deepening the kiss, and pulling Jack down to sit next to him on the hearth.

Savoring the dance of their tongues, Jack gradually became aware Aneurin's tongue was forked. Only slightly, but different nonetheless. It served as a constant reminder Aneurin wasn't human.

Both of them reached up to remove each other's clothing. The laces of Aneurin's tunic snapped in their haste.

They were forced to break the kiss so Aneurin could stand and lift his tunic off. His erection jutted clearly from his drawstring pants, right in front of Jack's face.

Jack gave up resisting his impulses. He bent to nuzzle the tempting bulge.

Aneurin shuddered once, then his hands lifted and his fingers combed through Jack's hair. "You can't know how good that feels, Jackie. Er, Jack."

Jack felt around the waist of Aneurin's pants. "Yes, I can. You can show me in a minute." He fumbled a bit more, and then gave up. "Soon as you show me how to get you out of those pants."

Aneurin grinned. "Let's do this the easy way. I find I'm eager." His clothes disappeared.

Jack blinked to find he nuzzled flesh, but he recovered in two seconds to swallow the delight in front of him. There'd be time enough to savor the taste once he got Aneurin on his back.

Aneurin groaned and threw his head back. His fingers clutched Jack's hair more firmly.

Jack's hands rested on Aneurin's hips. He slid them around to grasp Aneurin's ass and hold him firmly while he used his tongue to slide up the shaft of his cock with teasingly tight suction.

Aneurin's fingers tightened in his hair. "Oh, no, my handsome human friend. This time is meant for tasting viands slowly, not gulping them down greedily. You are still dressed. This I cannot allow to continue."

Jack hummed his humor, but allowed Aneurin to pull out of his mouth. He looked up the smooth expanse of broad chest. "Really? Then how can we rectify this?"

Aneurin chuckled. One hand swept through Jack's hair. "Since you already wisely removed your shirt, then you can either finish by divesting yourself of your pants, or I will shred them from your body."

Jack pretended to consider this. "Since I've no wish to have you return to dragon form any time soon, I suppose I'll just have to suffer." He stood and removed his pants, kicking them to one side. "Do I need to build up the fire?"

Aneurin's "No" was as soft as his hesitant touch on Jack's chest. "I ask for a final time, Jack. Are you sure of this?"

Jack understood the tentative nature of the question. "While I think it possible you're older than I by a good bit, I don't consider this a May-December affair." He reached out and pulled Aneurin into his arms. "Do you need further proof?"

"Yes." Aneurin waved toward his stone couch. "A great deal."

Jack laughed, and led Aneurin to the bed. "Then you'll have all you can handle." He stopped for a moment. "I, uh, suppose we don't have to worry about diseases transmitted dragon to human, so we can go bareback?"

Aneurin looked puzzled. "Bareback? You wish to ride me naked like this? Wouldn't you get cold?"

Jack snickered. "Sorry, Aneurin. Bareback is an expression that means we won't need to use condoms or..." He searched his memory for a term Aneurin would know. "French purses or sheep's bladders?"

Surprisingly, Aneurin blushed. "Oh! No, we cannot harm one another. Though, if you wish it, there is cooking oil to ease our way with one another."

Jack nodded, relieved. Saliva was very inadequate as a lubricant. "Good. I don't have anything on me."

Aneurin leered. "I noticed." He sat on the edge of his couch and reached for Jack. "Where were we?"

Jack evaded his questing hands. "I was giving you a blow job, but I've a mind to give you more, if you allow."

Aneurin frowned in puzzlement. "Blow job? Is that what they call it now? More? What more would you like?"

Jack grinned and crawled into the very center of the depression in the middle of the couch. "Good thing your dragon body kept this thing warm all this time. I'll teach you all the new terms for what I want to do as we go." He lay on his back. "Come straddle my face, with your knees pointing in the direction of my feet."

Aneurin blinked, and then complied. "I can suckle you this way as well. I like this."

"That's called a sixty-nine, but I'd like you to remain upright, please." Jack's grin of devilment grew wider.

Aneurin's balls, perineum, and ass were displayed above him, all within easy access. He vowed to go slowly. "Prepare yourself, my friend." He licked carefully and sensually at the seam on Aneurin's scrotum.

The dragon-man gasped and held his breath. "But I cannot pleasure you."

Jack ignored the strangled and haltingly spoken protest. The sweet taste of clean flesh tempted him more than banter. He sucked one deliciously hairless ball into his mouth, and then the other.

Aneurin trembled above him, his breathing whooshing out before filling his lungs again. "By the eggs of my foremothers, you'll drive me to madness this way."

Jack released the warm globes one by one. "I'm not done." His tongue caressed with minimal pressure the perineum, just to give Aneurin time to adjust to the new sensation.

Aneurin cried out and shuddered once.

The gasping half-shout was all the encouragement Jack needed or wanted. He licked and buried his nose in the secret place between balls and ass, where he tasted the clean spicy smell of Aneurin's true form.

Aneurin was still, but moaning. His ass puckered and released, like a tempting beacon.

Jack gave up resisting. He lifted his face away from the tang of dragon flesh. "And this is a rim job. Hope you like it." He licked around Aneurin's anus.

Aneurin roared a long, gasping sound that should not have come from so human-seeming a being. He writhed, but did not remove himself. "That feels... incredible, Jack. Please stop or our pleasures will be much shortened."

After one, long slow nibble on the underside of a firm, smooth ass cheek, Jack let him go.

Panting as if he lifted a ton to move each limb, Aneurin crawled off and fell to one side on his back. His cock jutted toward the ceiling, so distended it was nearly as purple as his natural form. "By all the eggs, Jack. You amaze me."

Jack chuckled and rolled off the couch. His ankle twinged, and he fought to stay upright. "Good. I intend to do more. Where's that oil, again?"

Aneurin cracked one eye. "In the cabinet, in a red bottle. What will you do with it?"

The bottle was in the very back of the darkest corner. Jack brandished it triumphantly. "The better for you to fuck me with, my dear... dragon."

* * *

Jack gimped back to the couch and crawled across until he knelt beside Aneurin. He admired how the man before him was in shape despite a certain thinness. The black and silver hair fanned out beneath Aneurin's head like an aura. The whiskey and milk eyes beckoned to his soul. He didn't believe the confident statements of how Aneurin could live without sight. His dragon was starving, and it broke his heart. They'd discuss it later.

Grasping the jutting, hot cock, he watched the dragon's eyes haze. Jack dribbled the oil with care not to waste what little there was.

Aneurin shut his eyes and breathed deeply. "You cannot know how I've longed for your touch, Jack. I thought you'd never return." His breathing quickened as Jack stroked the oil lazily up and down, covering every inch. "If I am dreaming, I refuse to awaken. If I am awake, then I wish never to sleep again."

Jack put the bottle of oil over the side of the couch, and let it slide down to land on a pile of dragon scales. "Same goes for me. No matter what, we can enjoy the here and now." He oiled his own ass, and climbed atop Aneurin.

Aneurin held himself still and allowed Jack to inch his way down at his own pace. His breath hissed as the head of his cock pressed past the first sphincter, but other than that one sound, he spoke not a word. His hands crept up and grasped Jack's hips to steady him.

Jack shut his eyes and allowed the delicious sensation of being filled to course through him. The fit was perfect. Not enough to cause pain, and not so little that his insides weren't gently and sweetly caressed. He threw back his head and slid a bit further down until the second sphincter was breached.

Aneurin's hands trembled on Jack's hips. "You feel so marvelous, Jack. I cannot bear much more."

Shuddering, Jack slid the last few inches down until Aneurin's cock was buried deep. His own cock ached with need, but Jack vowed to savor what he could of the sensations. He didn't want conversation right now -- he wanted a good fucking and intended to have it.

He began the ascent at a much faster pace, but still not the pounding jolts he longed for. "Shut up and fuck me. We'll discuss how good it was after."

Aneurin's eyes shut, and a draconic purring growl rolled out of his mouth. His hands tightened on Jack's hips and assisted him in moving ever faster.

This was the way Jack liked things to be done, with rhythmic movements that caressed his prostate mercilessly. He lifted one hand and clamped down on his own cock to pump and ease the aching need for a spurting orgasm.

Each down stroke brought moans from Jack and another growl from Aneurin. They locked in a tangle of sensations neither wanted to end and yet both craved release.

Aneurin growl-purred softly, and his thrusts upward took on the force of hammer blows, pounding into Jack's ass.

The short, hard strokes drove Jack close to the edge, but not over, until Aneurin reached up with a hand to pinch and tweak Jack's right nipple.

Jack came with a force he'd not known was possible, spurting thickly with agonizingly sweet shots.

Aneurin followed, roaring out his pleasure and slamming Jack down until Jack felt every jerking movement as his ass filled.

His balls empty, Jack fell forward, panting. He could barely get a breath before the next wave of pleasure overtook him.

Jack wanted to shout in triumph. He hadn't awakened, and he'd gotten the full pleasure he'd desired from his dreams without a fearful jolt upright in a dark and lonely bed. If he could have gotten a lungful of air, he might have whooped. The best he could do was lean down to tenderly kiss Aneurin's equally heaving chest.

They lay still and fought for breath until Aneurin's cock softened and slid out with one final caress.

Jack could have whimpered at the loss. More. He craved more.

Aneurin pulled Jack off until they cradled each other in a loving embrace. The dragon leaned over and kissed Jack, lingering and savoring. "After we've rested for a time, it will be my turn. Agreed?"

Too spent to do more than nod, Jack smiled to show his willingness.

Aneurin pulled him closer. "Agreed then. Thank you, Jack." His words ended on a yawn.

With his arm across Aneurin's ribs, he could feel the bones protruding. His dragon had been ill or starving, and most likely it was the latter. What had Jack done but make him burn more fuel than he could afford? Would Aneurin have enough reserve resources to hunt? Guilt insinuated itself in Jack's consciousness, and he winced. He had to know. "Aneurin?"

The "Hmm?" was a sleepy, satisfied murmur.

"I haven't worn you out too much, have I? You'll still be able to fly and hunt, right? I know you said if you got too hungry, you couldn't fly." Jack heard the worry in his own voice and prayed he didn't sound like a whining kid.

Sleepily, Aneurin chuckled. "Remembered that too, did you?" He kissed Jack's forehead. "You did feed me. You just don't know it." His next breath was a cross between a snore and a rumble.

Jack chuckled. "You can explain that statement when we wake up." He sighed contentedly and watched the sunlight play on the walls of the outer cavern. It must be late afternoon for a cave to get this much light. He wondered what time it was back in America. Late morning? Ah, well. It was Saturday. He could sleep in.

Aneurin rolled a little closer and pulled Jack in tighter to his body, so they nestled like spoons. The irony of having a Saturday lie-in with a dragon sleeping plastered up to his back didn't escape Jack's humor.

Well, no matter. Jack fully intended to enjoy this dream or whatever it was until he was forced out of it. He grinned and fervently wished he'd get another round with Aneurin before it all came crashing down.

If he were lucky, he'd sleep until Monday morning. Aneurin's body warmed his back, he was safe and not all that concerned with anything other than sliding his cock into a certain dragon's willing ass. He cradled his head on Aneurin's biceps to watch the play of sunlight and listen to the bells.

Wait.

What bells? Dread filled Jack's heart. It wasn't church bells. It was the ringing of his cell phone. "Aww, shit."

Aneurin raised his head, his milky eyes seeking danger instantly. "What? Where? Oh, no!"

Jack felt himself being yanked by the navel back to reality. The cave faded into mist. "No!" he cried out, hearing his voice echo and a despairing draconic roar in response before the world faded to black.

The jangling bells of his cell blared in his ear from the coffee table in his penthouse when Jack opened his eyes. He snarled with hatred at the phone and flung it angrily across the living room. It landed in a big ficus his decorator had suggested and plopped down into the generous pot out of sight. The ringing stopped.

Jack scrubbed the tears falling down his face with the back of his left hand and wished whoever had called a short ride to hell.

His watch sat on the coffee table like a recrimination of time wasted, its display citing the late morning hour. He snarled at it, too.

The empty brandy snifter had the audacity to sparkle in the light. Jack reached for the bottle and glass, considering drinking himself back into oblivion and Aneurin's arms if he could make it happen again.

Instead, the snifter sailed in the same general direction as the cell, with more destructive results. The shattering tinkle gave small vent to Jack's frustrations.

He sat up, resigned to a day of drudgery and the pile of paper waiting in his briefcase. The slight chill of the morning air had him shivering, and he reached for his shirt. His hand stopped questing. It was nowhere in sight. His jacket and tie were draped on the back of the sofa, just where he'd left them. His shoes and socks were under the coffee table. "Shit. I must have been drunker than I thought."

The ache blooming between his eyebrows warned him he'd better be prepared to drink a gallon of coffee or he'd never get a thing done. "Coffee first. Then I hunt for the shirt."

Jack stood, his eye on the large black commercial coffeemaker he'd bought to satisfy his addiction to caffeine and his late night hours. He grinned to himself, remembering he had set the timer before beginning his binge last night. The coffee inside that carafe could probably melt a metal spoon by now. Just the way he liked it.

A sharp pain shot from his left ankle up his leg, and Jack sat down hard on the sofa.

Now he was awake enough to notice he was naked. He'd gone to sleep clothed. His left ankle sported a very impressive bruise and a scabbed but recent scrape.

Jack wet his lips with his tongue and did a final internal check. He swallowed long and deep when he noted his ass was a little tender, then he began to grin.

Carefully, he rose once more to his feet and limped with slow, deliberate steps the long distance to his coffee pot. Automatically reaching for a mug, his hand pulled down his favorite black ceramic one with a purple dragon on it.

Chuckling, then laughing maniacally, Jack poured himself a generous serving of the dark brew.

He couldn't dance without falling on his ass, but his heart was doing a good job on its own.

"Real. It was real!" He limped over to pluck his phone from the planter. He couldn't wait to tell Dr. Lledrith.

He'd only punched the first three buttons when it dawned on him that the good doctor would surely lock him in a nice padded cell with an "I love me" jacket of his very own if he told the truth.

He erased the numbers and sat down at the dining table he normally used for a desk, shoving aside the litter of his latest project to make just enough room for his cup.

The memory of Aneurin's ribs sticking out like a horrific bas-relief made him grimace and slug more coffee down his throat. "What did you mean when you said I'd already fed you, Aneurin?"

He slammed his coffee down so hard the liquid sloshed over the rim and spattered onto one of the reports from his field supervisors on the Georgetown project. He idly brushed away the droplets and nodded thoughtfully. The project didn't seem so important anymore. Andy knew his wishes. One phone call, and Andy would be all over the project like white on rice.

Jack pulled a legal pad in front of him and began to make a list while he sipped from his rapidly cooling coffee. By the time the last drop made its icy way down his throat, Jack dialed the first call.

He drummed his fingers impatiently and waited. "Andy? Yeah, it's me, Jack Draper. Can you take over the Georgetown project? I have an emergency trip to make to Wales. Sick friend. No, I don't know how long I'll be. Thanks, Andy."

Smiling in satisfaction, Jack dialed his travel agent. He prayed he remembered the spellings. "Hey, Arlene. Jack Draper. I have a weird itinerary this time for you. Grab a pen. You'll need to write down some odd spellings. I'm going to Wales. Today."

Chapter Four

Jack studied the cliff below him and hefted the heavy wicker basket of fresh fish in his left hand. The rocks looked even more treacherous than he remembered, and his twisted ankle still throbbed from his walk through the village of Llansanffraid. Most of his luggage sat on the bed of his private leased guesthouse, and he hoped like hell he'd never need to use that room.

Both his hands were encumbered so he couldn't even rub his aching forehead. The right hand held a small gym bag full of tea, a tin of biscuits, a bottle of lube, and a few small sundries. Getting down the pile of rocks with the sea waves making them slick and wet was treacherous, even with his hands free. "I'm crazy. I must be. Great. Now I'm talking to myself, and all I had for breakfast was tea."

His stomach rumbled audibly and his head pounded from the lack of adequate caffeine. Now he wished he'd stayed for the hearty fry-up breakfast the local inn advertised in the window. The traditional British fried eggs, sausage links, beans, a fine thick round slab of British bacon, half a grilled tomato, toast, and hot tea. His mouth watered even as he imagined his arteries slamming shut.

Briefly, he considered giving up this foolish notion of climbing down sea-soaked rocks in hopes of feeding a dying blind dragon inside a cave. Dammit, it sounded worse when he put it that way.

The memory of Aneurin's anguished cry of despair countered all his logic. Jack squared his shoulders. "Time to see if I'm insane enough for a rubber room, or if I'm... oh, hell, I don't know anymore." He clambered down awkwardly onto the first rock and began his descent. He just hoped it wasn't into madness.

The climb was full of heart-stopping moments where he was sure he and his burdens would plunge headlong into the water, but he made it to the bottom with no further injuries. The pinkish granite boulder that allowed him to see the cavern entrance was there, just as he'd dreamed. He stomped on it, feeling somewhat like an idiot. Surely the greater weight of a fully-grown man stepping on it would be enough, but why take a risk?

He hadn't realized he was holding his breath until the air whooshed from his lungs at the appearance of the cavern entrance. The last hop over to the ledge caused his ankle to twinge, but at least he didn't fall on his ass and lose the fish back to the sea.

Everything was just as he'd dreamt so far, but he couldn't bring himself to call out like his heart demanded with ever-increasing volume. He felt like a fool enough as it was. The water-smoothed walls of the cavern glittered faintly, with the sun obscured by the cliff. Jack nodded, ticking off the list of dream memories. "Okay, maybe I'm not a complete lunatic. But is this just a cave from a child's memory of imaginary adventures, or is there really a dragon in here?" He drew a ragged breath. "One way to find out."

His feet felt like lead weights, reluctantly taking him to the darkened back of the cavern. The black maw of an opening was there, just out of sight of the main entrance. Jack swallowed a gulp of saliva to wet his dry throat. There was no beacon of sparkling lights to guide him. The unlit back cave was an unwelcoming pit of darkness.

He put down the stinking basket of fish and rummaged in the gym bag for the Mag-Lite he'd flown over in his suitcase. It had come in handy many a time to explore properties where no electricity worked, and this was another such case where he'd need its light to see what was hidden in the dark. Jack snorted to himself at the irony. Most of the time when he used the flashlight, he hoped he wouldn't find something. This time, he sincerely hoped he would.

The mere twisting of the handle and the comforting beam lighting the sandy cavern floor gave him courage.

He picked up the gym bag, but left the fish where they were. If he was wrong, he couldn't bear the thought of standing in an empty cave with nothing more than a basket of fish to catch his broken dreams.

With one deep breath to fortify himself, he stepped into the blackness and swept the beam around the room. The fireplace full of ashes with the rusty kettle still on the hook reassured him.

More, the light reflected off something that glittered darkly in the shadows to his left. Purple dragon scales at eye level. His hand trembled when no movement of breath reassured him of Aneurin's continued life.

The gym bag and flashlight hit the floor with a soft thud. Jack ran forward with his heart in his throat, ignoring the scream of his ankle at the abuse. A warm puff of air blew his sweater against his chest and ruffled his hair. It was laden with the smell of dead fish.

Jack choked and coughed. Relief suffused his whole being, even while his heart still pounded. "Whoa, you need a case of Tic-Tacs, carrion breath. Wake up, Aneurin."

One whiskey-gold eye opened and studied him. The other eye flew open, bathing Jack in a glittering light. "J-J-Jack?"

Laughing with happiness at this sign that his friend lived, Jack threw his arms wide. "The one and only. In the flesh. This is no dream." He walked over and kissed Aneurin on the nose, right between the two flaring nostrils.

Something long and thin wrapped around his waist.

Jack squirmed when something dipped down and tickled his crotch. "If that's your tongue, I've better uses for it."

"The better to taste you with, m'dear." Aneurin's mind voice was un-muffled by the forked appendage's occupation with caressing Jack's jeans.

Jack chuckled. "I've something better for you to taste than a gamy human." He deliberately changed his tone to insinuating. "At least for now."

"If that's the fish I smell, I'll take it. They smell marvelous." The forked tongue left Jack's waist.

Jack discreetly touched his sweater. Dry as a bone. He didn't fancy the slimy feeling of tongue saliva in that large amount, so he was grateful Aneurin was a reptile.

The lit outer cave was easy enough to find, since the Mag-Lite currently illuminated a small patch of sand and nothing more. Jack limped out and retrieved the basket.

When he turned around, the inner cavern was ablaze with illuminated crystals. He walked back in, breathing a sigh of relief to see everything just as he'd dreamt. "Someday, I'd love to find out how you light your cavern."

"I might tell you. Later. Is that a salmon I smell?" Aneurin hadn't moved off the couch, nor changed to human form, but his eyes were alight with interest.

Jack grinned and lifted the requested fish by the tail. "The largest I could purchase off the only fishmonger open at this early hour." He tossed it to Aneurin.

The dragon jaws snapped the fish in one gulp. "Delicious, and almost as fresh as I could catch myself. I'm as hungry as a hatchling suddenly. Hope that basket is full."

Jack picked up the next fish in the pile and threw it. "It is indeed, my friend. I hope you've a full belly of fire. I've a pile of firewood to be brought down later for our mutual comfort. The deliveryman thought me quite odd when I told him I wanted a full cord of wood above our heads on the cliff, until I lied and said I planned a bonfire with a few friends."

A small snort produced a trickle of flame from each nostril of Aneurin's snout. "I'll be more than full after this meal." He snapped the third offering Jack tossed. "We'll go up and get enough to last until dark, then we can load the rest on my back and bring the whole pile down at once. I've a net around here somewhere I can carry in my claws." His eyes half closed. "That's the best method for now."

Jack paused and bobbled the last fish, almost dropping it to the sands. He caught the stinking thing and put it directly in Aneurin's mouth. "That sounds like there's another way."

The dragon swallowed. "Well, yes, but I'd rather put off talking about it. Would you mind?"

Shrugging, Jack went to wash his hands free of the stench of fish at the fountain. "I've a thousand other questions. Seems only proper to ask them all at once." He turned and found his shirt he'd left before. It made an adequate towel, and he doubted he'd wear it again. "Remind me to bring a few better linens when I next go back to the village, would you? I've leased a cottage for the week, so they won't think it odd of me to do a bit of shopping, even if I have to drive to Aberystwyth."

Aneurin's human voice now came from the couch. "I'll try. What's that torch thing on the floor?"

"The Mag-Lite." Jack picked up the flashlight and turned it off. He stuffed it back in the gym bag and found his PDA. "Let me see if I can make a list." He pulled out the stylus. "Towels, table, chairs, tins of food, can opener. Damn, I should have brought my camping gear. Ah, well, I'll pick up new. Anything else you can think of?" For the first time, he lifted his gaze and looked directly at Aneurin.

His friend lay naked in his human form upon the great couch, grinning. No blanket covered him. "More cooking oil?"

Jack matched the leer with one of his own. "Sure, but I've something much better in my bag for the purposes I intend."

His drawled insinuation had the desired effect. Aneurin's face lit with interest. "Something modern like that odd metal quill and parchment in your hand?"

Glancing down at the PDA, Jack chuckled and shut it off. "Yes. I'll show this to you later. I've much to show you, if you can keep your form for a long time." He stowed the PDA in the gym bag, then carried it over to sit next to Aneurin. "A great deal to show you, if you wish."

The dragon man tossed his hair out of the way and cupped Jack's face in his hand. "I can keep this form as long as I wish, only returning to my true state when unconscious or dead."

Jack leaned forward until his lips were inches from their goal of Aneurin's eagerly awaiting mouth. He was relieved to note there was no fish smell on Aneurin's breath now that he was human. "Then don't die anytime soon, please." He brushed his lips tenderly over his friend's. "However, I intend to fuck us both to near unconsciousness, if you're as willing as I am."

One of those sexy draconic purrs answered him. "We've time until sunset. I'm sure we can keep each other warm and occupied until then." However, instead of moving in closer, Aneurin pulled away and stood.

Surprised by the sudden movement, Jack let him go. He was unsure of himself, and didn't know how to proceed. "What's the matter? Aren't you interested?"

Awkwardly, Aneurin scuffed the sand. "I remember your promise, you see. Well, I have to return to dragon form for a moment. I do have a belly full of fire, and if I don't release some of the extra air, I might... well, scorch your tenderest parts."

Jack choked and tried not to laugh. The picture he conjured in his mind was too funny. "So, draconic digestion means the gas can come out fiery at either end, I take it."

Blushing, Aneurin looked a trifle offended. "Well, yes. The... gas, you called it... alights automatically when it comes outside my body. Works better coming out my mouth, though. We chew on certain rocks that make it catch fire. Very tasty, as a matter of fact. But they do pass out of the body eventually, and some might cause the other end to alight."

Jack snickered. He couldn't help it. Dragon farts that caught on fire were just too amusing. "Well, then, I suppose you'd better get on with it. Better out than remaining in your system."

"I'm so very glad you find it amusing. You wouldn't if I scorched your cock to a blackened sausage." Aneurin sniffed huffily and changed form.

His lips twitching, Jack waited attentively for what was likely to be a spectacular sight. "Long as you don't shit a rock anytime soon, I can deal with this little…" he choked down laughter, "… ceremonial moment."

Aneurin haughtily backed his ass up until his tail literally wound out the cavern entrance. The sound that followed reminded Jack of the old gas furnace at the orphanage catching on -- a rush of air, then a *whump* of ignition. The outraged shriek of a gull seemed the perfect ending.

That cry of a singed gull was the last straw for Jack. He collapsed on the dragon couch, guffawing at dragon farts.

An outraged dragon's roar startled him almost as much as the launch of Aneurin's full dragon body, which landed directly atop him. The only things that saved Jack from being crushed were the four claws scrabbling for a hold on the edges of the couch.

Jack held his breath, and stared into Aneurin's golden eyes.

"So, you think I'm funny. Am I so amusing now?" the angry dragon's voice rumbled in his mind.

* * *

Blinking, Jack tried to make the adjustment from his loving friend to angry dragon. It just didn't compute. He stared into the milky gold eyes of

Aneurin and thought he detected humor, though it was difficult to read any emotion from a dragon.

More to the point, something long and very firm lay on the inside of his right foot. He rubbed it with his sneaker-clad foot and felt the purr deep in Aneurin's belly.

Jack grinned in triumph and kissed the purple muzzle looming over him. He deliberately made his voice low and enticing, hoping for a bit of shock value. "Oh, baby. I love it when you're forceful." He rubbed again. "Give me some hot smutty dominance, big guy."

Aneurin blinked, and his jaw fell open a trifle. "Jack! I'm… surprised at you!"

Swallowing laughter at the success of his trick, Jack confined himself to caressing Aneurin's huge draconic cock with his foot. "So am I. I'm usually the one in charge of the show. Shut up and change back to human. I don't fancy trying to work around your tail to find what I want."

Haughtily, Aneurin snorted a trickle of flame. "We mate on the wing, and you're not equipped for that." He changed form, returning to his previous nude state and rolled to lie beside Jack, grinning. "So, what are you waiting for? Moonrise?"

Eagerly, Jack sat up. Aneurin's hands plucked at his sweater. Jack obligingly lifted his arms to help with the removal while he toed off his shoes. He yanked off his socks and dropped them off the edge of the couch to land on top of his Nikes.

"You humans certainly wear a lot of clothes." Aneurin casually tossed the sweater in the same general direction as the athletic shoes.

Jack laughed and stood. The sand was cool beneath his bare feet, and he shifted back and forth from one foot to another while he unbuckled his belt and dropped his jeans around his ankles. He shivered in the cool air. "We feel the cold much more than you think, since we don't have scales and thick skin."

As soon as he tugged his turtleneck over his head and couldn't see, Aneurin attacked his underwear. "What is this bright red codpiece you're wearing, and where is the string to remove it?"

The turtleneck caught on Jack's ears, and muffled his chuckle. He fought himself free of the garment, and tossed it on the haphazard pile. He was both amazed and amused that Aneurin was so innocent of the changes in the world. Yes, it somehow was appropriate that a dragon remained so medieval in his outlook. "It's called a thong, my friend, and it will slide down."

Aneurin eyed the underwear dubiously. "Thong is right. It is little more than a scrap of cloth and string. Why do you bother?"

Wiggling his eyebrows, Jack guided Aneurin's hand to the thong. "For the pleasure it brings others, in both displaying and concealing at the same time. I wore this for you."

The dragon's hand caressed the silk holding Jack's erect cock, and his eyes hazed with unrestrained lust. "I see." He leaned forward for a kiss, and his hand traced the outline of Jack's raging hard on with more confidence.

Jack bent down to meet him halfway without a thought, pouring himself into the kiss he'd wanted -- no, needed! -- for so long. Not the kisses shared half-heartedly between fuck-buddies or to appease an appetite, but the sharing of two lovers.

A large, rough hand with long hard nails slid between Jack's thong and hip. Aneurin hummed deep in his throat without breaking the delightful warring of their tongues.

Jack let Aneurin fight with the spandex for a moment, and then helped him remove the thong's pouch from his hardened cock.

Aneurin broke the kiss and moved back, his hands still fighting to slide the thong off Jack's hips. He looked up at Jack's face, or at least in that general direction, since Jack wasn't sure how much he could see. "Not as easy as you made it seem."

Admiring his lover on the couch was easy for Jack. He doubted Aneurin truly understood how beautiful he was, with his purplish-veined cock jutting arrow-straight at Jack, like a compass needle. In his human form, Aneurin's body may have been sculpted out of a gay man's fantasy, virtually hairless and proud, but his draconic nature showed in small things, like the purple tint to nipples and cock. Unusual, but not cartoon-like. Jack definitely didn't want to make love to a human version of a certain purple dinosaur children's icon.

He straightened up and put his hands on his hips, knowing his erection displayed better that way, as an enticement. "If you weren't reclining there looking like something out of a fantasy, then you'd have less difficulty."

The dragon's eyes lit with mischief, and he chuckled. "I remind you I *am* something out of a fantasy."

His thong at his knees, Jack started to reach down and remove it. Aneurin's hand stopped him.

"I like the idea of you trapped in a red string and pouch. Come here." The dragon reached to catch one of his nails in the thong and pulled Jack forward until his toes contacted the edge of the stone couch. The tips of Aneurin's tongue flickered out, tasting the air and then licking his lips.

At first, Jack wasn't sure what to do. Part of him rebelled at being commanded, and part of him melted like wax. The part that favored finding out what a forked dragon tongue could do won out.

Aneurin's black and silver hair obscured his facial expression, but his tongue reached what for a human would be an impossible length and wrapped around Jack's balls. The tips tickled beneath, halfway to Jack's ass.

His eyes half closed with delight, Jack fisted his hand in Aneurin's hair to give himself a balance point. "I could get to like dragon tongue."

The aforementioned appendage unwrapped itself slowly, lingering to taste every inch before retracting completely. Aneurin's breath teased Jack's cock head. "Here's human flesh before me. Meat to taste but never to bite. Now I know why my ancestors gained a fondness for humans." He growl-purred a sound that shouldn't have come from a human-like throat. "Delicious."

Shuddering, Jack felt the first scrape of sharp dragon teeth. He slid down Aneurin's throat, and felt the heat within. Intellectually, he knew it was the fires not yet lit in Aneurin's fire-breathing equipment, but the sensation was much more than the clinical analysis. He moaned on the end of a sigh, and let himself just experience.

Aneurin took his time, seeming to savor every moment of the in and out movement, using his teeth gently to cause pinpricks of pain while his tongue caressed or flicked out to give Jack a brief rim job.

Rimming was admittedly Jack's weakness, both giving and receiving. The sensation was so sensual, like an intimate invasion of the most sensitive and private area on the human body. A prelude of things to come that hinted of further pleasures.

Jack's breath caught in his throat with every downstroke until he was sure he'd lose control and cut his cock on Aneurin's razor teeth. "Heels in the air, dragon. You're due for this fucking."

Wordlessly and taking his time, Aneurin released him. He looked up at Jack triumphantly. His eyes glittered and the tips of his tongue licked his lips. He fell on his back slowly, purring, and pulled his knees under his chin.

Jack kept his eyes locked on his dragon's golden gaze. The gym bag was still open, and he found the bottle of lubricant by touch alone. The top popped open with a push of his thumb, and he warmed a few drops in his hand. It wouldn't be polite to slather the icy substance on anyone, much less a cold-sensitive creature.

He dipped his fingers into the puddle in his palm and gently applied it to Aneurin's exposed ass. His index finger teased until it slipped in with the superior slide of the lubricant, all the way to the second knuckle.

Aneurin's eyes half shut and his breathing hitched. The growling purr increased in volume.

The second finger worked its way in until it joined the first. Jack wondered at Aneurin's ease of acceptance. Humans had to work to open up so easily. His mind supplied the insane image of dragon-sized butt plugs. This time, he choked down the laughter before even one sound escaped.

Aneurin moaned. "Don't stop, Jack. That feels so very good, I cannot describe it."

Obediently, Jack worked in a third finger. Good God, was it possible to fist a dragon? He didn't want to find out. Fisting wasn't one of his kinks, though he had plenty.

Aneurin writhed at the finger fucking and his purring increased in volume until Jack couldn't hear the surf outside the cavern. "Now, Jack. Now."

Now there was a command he'd happily obey. Jack removed his fingers as caringly as he'd inserted them, and used the remainder of the lubricant to cover his cock and coax it back to full hardness with a few strokes. Not that he needed much! The sight of Aneurin's beauty and willing body would turn gelatin rock solid, as far as Jack was concerned. He paused at the entrance to Aneurin's ass, for one second concerned about the very real danger of losing his most precious commodity. The idea of losing his cock and nuts to a dragon fart brought him close to the edge of laughter, but at the same time carried a real fear.

The dragon purr reached a new intensity. It had a hypnotic quality and yet conveyed urgency.

Jack gave in to that plea and thrust slowly forward, determined to be gentle if it meant taking the next hour for the first downstroke.

Accepting his cock effortlessly, Aneurin's body pulled him deeper.

God, it was like fucking a velvet-lined furnace, hot but not burning. Jack's instinct to shove in until he was buried to the balls multiplied. He fought the urge with all his will until Aneurin's body opened to him fully. Then, and only then, did he give vent to the need.

Aneurin's purr never wavered from the intense, pleading tone, even when Jack drove in with unrestrained lust. He growled one word around the vibration in his throat. "Morrre!"

The exhilaration overwhelmed Jack. He shoved and pounded until his rasping breaths drowned out even the loud purrs and growls from Aneurin. He could feel his balls rise in preparation for one hell of a screaming orgasm.

The tone of the purr changed, and the dragon's eyes glowed. Aneurin's long hard nails analogous to dragon claws scraped shallow furrows in the hard granite of the couch, with a screech that resembled nails on a chalkboard.

Jack shouted his growing need to blow his wad deep into that hot center of his dragon lover's being. He wanted them to come together, but he couldn't gather the strength to lift one hand from Aneurin's knees where he'd braced himself, no matter how much he wanted to tweak one purplish-brown nipple below him.

Maybe his wish to do so was enough, because Aneurin's growl crescendoed to a roar, and the dragon-man's jism spattered on his belly and chest like a fountain.

Hoping he wouldn't put out Aneurin's internal fire with the force of his own orgasm, Jack came. And came. With every thrust, he shuddered with a renewed wave and wondered if he'd just go ahead and turn inside out.

Now Aneurin's lower legs became all the support that held Jack upright. His own knees threatened to buckle and collapse. Both remained where they were, fighting for breaths into air-starved and overworked bodies. Aneurin was the first to move, even if it was nothing more than to lift his hand and grasp Jack's left palm.

Jack managed to get his voice to work, though it came out as a harsh rasp. "God, that was incredible. I felt like I could fly." He felt himself soften enough to withdraw with one gentle tug.

Aneurin's milky-gold eyes were half-lidded. He smiled gently and pulled Jack's willing body into his arms. "You can. I'll teach you when we awaken. Sleep now."

Jack sensed a commanding force. It rose up and snatched consciousness from him before he could ask what the hell Aneurin meant.

Chapter Five

Flying his Cessna always gave Jack a thrill like nothing else. The plane was small enough to feel the wind and react to it, for good or bad. He soared and felt the wind in his face.

Wait a minute. Wind? Inside a plane?

And what was that heavy weight across his hips?

Panicked, his heart racing, Jack sat up. The icy chill of a Welsh evening breeze slapped him fully to consciousness.

Aneurin slept peacefully beside him, a sweet smile of contentment creasing his face. His arm draped gracefully over Jack's hips.

Jack's bladder screamed for mercy. Like it or not, he was forced to leave the warmth of Aneurin's arms. "Hope you have a toilet, Aneurin."

One golden eye cracked open. The sleepy mumble sounded like "No. Use the sea."

A distant ache in his hip reminded Jack that he wasn't used to sleeping on stone. He shoved at Aneurin's arm until the dragon man rolled over, muttering.

Mischief made Jack want to bite the ass now on display, but his bladder screamed louder. "I'll get you, my pretty, and your round little ass too." A huge shiver hit him. He scrambled for his clothes and all but ran for the cavern entrance, praying the magic protecting the cave from casual visitors would ensure privacy, even if the sun were down.

A few minutes later, Jack sighed in relief and flexed his ankle. If he wanted a fire for a cup of tea, he'd have to climb the rocks and bring some wood for the fireplace down. Grumbling to himself, he wished fervently for a phone. He chuckled and imagined that kind of call. "Hello, pizza delivery? Yeah, I want two large five meats with extra cheese. Just drop them over the side of this Welsh cliff southwest of Llansanffraid. Here's my credit card number and add twenty bucks for the sheer weirdness of this request."

With a resigned sigh, Jack went back in for the fish basket. Aneurin blinked sleepily at him, but the smile he gave Jack was so full of love, it made up for the seeming laziness.

Jack grinned and blew him a kiss. "I'm going to get us some firewood for tea. Be right back." He mockingly shook his finger at Aneurin. "Then, Lucy, you got some 'splaining to do."

Aneurin sat up. "Huh? My name's not Lucy. That's your mother's name."

Jack's jaw figuratively hit the floor while the basket did so literally. His emotions rolled and eddied like the sea crashing outside. Uppermost was a combination of anger and elation that defied description. Anger that Aneurin had kept a secret, and elation that somewhere Jack did have a mother. He choked out, "I'm going for the wood." He snatched up the basket and ran.

On the climb up, Jack's mind wrapped around the facts inherent in Aneurin's statement.

One, he'd used present tense, implying Jack's mother was alive.

Two, not only was she alive, but Aneurin knew her.

Three, her name was Lucy. Jack blinked as images of the famous American redhead, now long dead, flickered in his mind's eye.

Jack reached the top of the cliff and gathered a few cut logs. The new axe he'd paid for lay near the pile, so he spent a little of his excess of emotion chopping and shaving a bit of kindling. By the time he had a fair pile, his emotions made more sense.

"I'm angry because Aneurin knew about my mother and didn't tell me straight away, but not very. After all, I vowed I didn't need or want parents who didn't want me." He picked up the basket full of wood and kindling and made the descent.

Aneurin, now fully dressed with his hair tidily pulled back in a tail, waited with the kettle by the hearth. He kept his gaze fixed on the sand beneath his boots. "I've a great deal to explain, don't I?"

He looked so forlorn Jack's anger melted a bit more. Aneurin had always been an extremely forthright fellow, so there had to be a good explanation. "I'll assume I'll hear the reasons why along with the information, right?"

Aneurin glanced at Jack and seemed heartened. "You're not furious?"

Laying the kindling and logs out carefully, Jack shrugged. "I am a bit. There's no sense lying about it." He gestured to the small pyramid of kindling and sticks. "Would you mind?"

Aneurin started and bent forward. His breath came out in a controlled jet and ignited the pile effortlessly.

Jack threw on a larger log and waited for it to catch fire. "Look, this is awkward. You may as well spill it all."

Water splashed at his feet. Jack looked up to see Aneurin dumping the contents of the kettle on the sand, shrugging. "I don't see how this is going to help. I thought you wanted tea."

Jack slapped his hands on his forehead and tried not to laugh aloud. "No, Aneurin. To 'spill it' is an

American expression that means to tell all one knows. I do want tea."

Looking nonplussed, Aneurin absorbed the definition. "Oh." He returned to the fountain and refilled the kettle. "I promise to tell all I know. No more secrets." He came back and put the kettle over the merrily burning fire. "I just don't know where to begin."

A gravelly feminine voice came from the outer cave. "Why not start at the beginning?"

Both males leapt to their feet.

Dr. Lledrith stepped into the lit cavern, smiling and carrying a large picnic basket. "Looks like I timed my entrance well. I've brought dinner."

Jack stood with his mouth agape. "Dr. Lledrith. What are you doing here?"

His voice was drowned out by Aneurin's joyous shout. "Mother!"

Aneurin ran to hug Dr. Lledrith and relieve her of the basket.

Dr. Lledrith looked around the cavern and sniffed her disapproval. "Aneurin, didn't I teach you to keep a few amenities around for our humans? Make a table this instant. I'll not sit on the sands like a barbarian."

The air stirred, and a slight tingling raced through Jack's feet. A large, intricately carved oak table appeared, complete with a black iron candelabra.

Dr. Lledrith put her picnic basket on the table, and unloaded a veritable feast, including a wine bottle and glasses.

Jack cleared his throat. His mind was whirling with information that refused to sort into logical order. Ironic that he, a successful entrepreneur, couldn't seem to add a few simple facts together. Most prominent was the fact that Dr. Lledrith was Aneurin's mother. That was the only thing that made logical sense in his mind, and it shouldn't. "What's the occasion, Dr. Lledrith?"

Dr. Lledrith turned on a sympathetic smile and handed him a glass of wine. "I'd ask you to call me by my real name of Draig, but we can keep to what you know for now. I'll spare my son the awkwardness of an explanation and tell you myself, since he appears struck dumb. Won't you sit down?"

"I'm not struck dumb, Mother. I'm annoyed. Why are you involving yourself?" Aneurin took the wine his mother set in front of him and drained it in one gulp.

A fire flashed in Dr. Lledrith's eyes. The crisp snap in her voice made Jack shudder and believe she really was an annoyed dragoness. "Because Jack was beginning to suffer from your ill-conceived spell and you were dying because of your pride, that's why! Lucynda and I are your mothers, and we won't stand idly by, scrying in the mirror while you two fools make a mess of it."

Jack blinked. Another piece of a very large puzzle. What ill-conceived spell?

* * *

Jack had a feeling all would come out in the wash. He did agree that calling her Dr. Lledrith was easier on his already overloaded brain. He had another question to ask first. One that seemed more important. "Uh, ma'am? I take it you know my mother?"

"She's your mother's dragon," Aneurin muttered. The dragon-man's hand clasped Jack's free hand. "Just as I'm yours."

Jack swallowed and absorbed the implication. "My mother is a lesbian?"

Dr. Lledrith snorted. "Do sit down, the pair of you! I'm getting a crick in my neck looking up at you. I'm bisexual, as most dragons are. Yes, your mother is lesbian, or I wouldn't have soul-bonded with her."

Jack and Aneurin sat as one, still holding hands.

Dr. Lledrith passed them each a sandwich and opened a bag of potato chips. "Aneurin, do you mind if I start the tale?"

Aneurin stood to dig into the basket for paper plates and loaded two with chips. "Go ahead, Mother. You know this part better than I."

Deciding he'd better keep his mouth shut, Jack bit into the roast beef and cheese. Maybe some of the questions whirling around in his brain would be answered before he asked.

Dr. Lledrith took a plate and a large handful of chips. "I do love these things. Can't get them in Honalee. I keep trying to persuade your mother, but she won't hear of it. They are very bad for us, and we don't need any more vices. So, I take them back with me whenever I visit this place." She grinned at Jack. "I'm a very spoiled dragon, and I know it."

Jack nodded. "Okay, you and my mother live in Honalee, and at least one of you can do magic like mirror scrying."

Dr. Lledrith beamed and shoved the ketchup toward Aneurin's questing hand. "I do love your ordered mind. Yes, your mother is the Red Sorceress of Honalee. Dragons can't scry. That's why Aneurin lost touch with you."

An unintelligible mumble around the sandwich in Aneurin's mouth sounded like, "That and other reasons."

"Who's telling this tale? You or me? You'll get your turn. And don't talk with your mouth full." She passed out paper napkins as if she sat down to picnics in seaside dragon caves all the time.

Maybe she did. Jack shrugged. "And my father? I assume I do or did have one."

She sniffed. "Of course you do. Lucy and I decided we wanted offspring and set out to hunt up our mates. I found mine first. You humans complicate matters, so it took her longer. I'd laid my egg before she could finish her negotiations with a minor mage named Cadell. Aneurin hatched the same month you were conceived." She frowned. "We never expected Cadell to go back on his word. He tried to steal you the night you were born."

Jack's sandwich stopped its progress to his mouth. "He tried to steal me? Why?"

Aneurin broke in. "Mage-born children are valuable. Blood mages use them in sacrifices to gain enormous power." He paused. "Cadell was a blood mage. He hid that very well from Lucynda."

Dr. Lledrith's smile was smug. "But not from her dragon. As you can well imagine, we can smell it on them. I'd not had a chance to meet him before Aneurin hatched, and I was occupied keeping him fed until the night of your birth." She shuddered. "If I hadn't been there, helping your mother, he might have stolen you with no one the wiser. I smelled something bloody where none should be and snapped out. I got his leg and broke his invisibility spell. Disgusting taste. I spat out that leg, and he flew out the window, screaming."

"Unfortunately, he lived." Aneurin's growl and clenched fist expressed his anger. "Now he wanted revenge more than he wanted you."

Dr. Lledrith reached across the table and patted Aneurin's hand. "Calm down, dear." She kept her hand on top of Aneurin's, but turned a bleak gaze on

Jack. "We managed to keep you hidden until the age of five. Then you were a little boy with more mischief than a crate of gryphonettes. Cadell was going to succeed unless we found a better place to hide you. We chose this world."

Aneurin sighed. "I'm sorry to say I wasn't ready to soul bond with you. Dragons mature a little more slowly. They sent me back in time so I'd have the years I'd need to grow, learn to fly, and be a proper dragon guardian."

Jack blinked and cleared his throat. "So, I was put on this -- world. Alone?"

"Nonsense! Here, have another sandwich, and eat some chips. I've cakes and honey for dessert."

Aneurin perked up. "Honey?"

Jack dredged up the memory that dragons were often given honey as an offering when a sacrifice wasn't available. Legend had it dragons loved honey, and Aneurin's greedy interest seemed to confirm it. He remembered how Dr. Lledrith had ladled honey in her coffee. Wait. Coffee. Now his eyes lit up. "Um, ma'am? Did you happen to bring coffee for a caffeine-deprived human?"

"Oh, yes. Sorry, dear. It's freeze-dried, but this should do." She reached in the basket and tossed a jar of instant at him. A paper cup suitable for hot liquids followed.

Jack dropped his sandwich and managed to catch both. "Instant is better than nothing. Thank you." He gratefully made himself a cup at the hearth. "Please continue, Dr. Lledrith. I take it I was cared for, at least at first."

"Yes, by me. However, we hadn't counted on two things. One, the world here had changed so that the gold your mother sent me would be questioned by the authorities, and two that you had already achieved a light soul bond with Aneurin, your playmate. As soon as I was arrested for gold trafficking, you set off to find Aneurin. The fact that you were only five and couldn't speak a word of this world's languages didn't even dawn on you."

He could see it clearly. A small boy and a baby dragon, wandering a city at night, alone. He shuddered. "My God!"

Aneurin cleared his throat. "The humans found you three days later. Someone had fed you, but, well, there's no delicate way to put this. You'd been -- what do they call it now? -- sodomized?"

* * *

Dr. Lledrith sobbed into her paper napkin. "I failed you, dear. They kept me in that tiny cell where I couldn't transform. Your mother's mirror was back at my flat, so she was frantic, and without me to transport her between the worlds, she was stuck in Honalee. They kept me many days, and by then you were gone."

A dark room and half-remembered terror flickered through Jack's mind. He looked down to see his fists clenched and white-knuckled. "I don't remember much of it, truthfully. Not consciously. I hope they caught whoever did it."

Aneurin snarled. "They buried the remains, anyway. I heard your pain through our soul bond. I shouldn't have, not from that distance in time, but I did. Then I did something no one thought possible for a fledgling. I came to you and shredded him." Aneurin flexed his claws, and shredded his sandwich to a mess of tatters. He shook his head. "Two younglings who shouldn't be alone, one injured and one a supposedly mythical beast. I couldn't change to human form then.

We were lucky I fit through the door. I got you out, and that was the best I could do."

Dr. Lledrith lifted her face from her napkin. "Our two babies, alone in that horrid place. Aneurin had sense enough to hide in an alley in a trash bin come morning, but you cried when he went out of sight." She gulped down wine. "We were very lucky in a way. Your sobs brought a policeman. He took one look and scooped you up."

Aneurin sighed. "There was nothing I could do except watch. I knew humans must not discover me. I had to let him take you away, and pray the soul bond would help me find you again."

Jack dredged up a wisp of humor, though the horror of this revelation still had his heart pounding. He knew it was the truth, even without memory of the incident. "My dragon spent a night in a trash bin for me. No greater love than that."

Aneurin put down the remains of his sandwich and grimaced. "I spent a lot of nights in trash bins and ate so many rats I can't bear to look at one even now. It took me months to locate you. By then, Mother had found me, but not you. We had to depend on my thread-thin contact with you."

Jack frowned. "Why didn't Dr. Lledrith simply change to human and ask for the whereabouts of a missing boy of my description?"

Dr. Lledrith had regained some of her aplomb. "They wouldn't tell me. I had no proof you were mine, and you were already abused and in shock. I didn't even have an address anymore, much less a telephone."

He could see that. Jack shuddered. "No identification, no address, and a police record. To say the least, they wouldn't let you near me."

Aneurin's hand covered his. "Until your mind came back, I couldn't find you either. Mother took over my lessons, here in this cave. She brought your mother here several times, and together they constructed the protections that kept us safe. They didn't dare do it often, because Cadell watched them." He drew a long, sighing breath. "You awoke from your shock trance a few months later, and we rejoiced. You were right there at the orphanage, with a new name and new life. Cadell couldn't find you except through our mothers."

Dr. Lledrith picked up the tale, though there was a catch in her breath. "We had to leave you there. Cadell had shared sex with your mother, and through her could home in on me. Only Aneurin could guard you and keep you safe. We had to abandon you both to grow up in the human world together." She rubbed her forehead with shaking hands. "Meanwhile, I set about trying to establish a human identity. It took me a long time."

He could figure out the rest. He knew the human world, since he was one. "You chose the profession of therapist in hopes that I might need some counseling as a formerly abused orphan. But it took too long to get the degree and establish yourself, didn't it?"

"It wasn't tea and crumpets, but it was worth it in the end." Dr. Lledrith had a right to the pride in her voice. A dragoness who didn't speak English had managed to establish a full legal identity and get a degree in a difficult subject concerning a race other than her own.

The emotions he'd been expecting hit him like a tidal wave. Jack trembled and fought for some measure of control. The roaring in his ears wasn't the soft sounds of the surf, but the wind-shredded howl of a hurricane. He shut his eyes. Memories of a dark room, an industrial green emergency room, and the beige walls of the orphanage's dorm room skittered across his brain like a bad horror film. The disjointed images made little sense.

A warm hand closed over his, providing him with an anchor point. He seized the lifeline with gratitude, and the roaring ceased.

Aneurin's hazy eyes were full of concern and fear, so Jack dredged up a smile. "I'm all right. This is a great deal to absorb."

Aneurin shot one glance at his mother's stony face.

Dr. Lledrith waved her hand. "Get it over with, son. Jack can take one more bit of trauma before we take him home."

Jack's head shot up. Visions of going back to his penthouse alone to sort through this mess were too much to bear. And there was more? "Home? No, not yet."

He had yet to deal with the concept of having a mother. The very thought of meeting this Lucynda made him break out in a cold sweat, and yet made his heart yearn. He needed time to think, but not alone. At that very moment, all he wanted was to bury his face in Aneurin's chest and stop thinking for a few hours.

Her face remained cold. "Let's see how you feel when you hear the rest. Then we'll make some decisions."

Aneurin huffed out a breath. "How much of your eighteenth birthday do you remember, Jack?"

Ah. Here was the crux of the matter. Something had happened around that time. "I've been dreaming of coming to you here, holding my college acceptance letter. You were upset, but we made love I think. I challenged you into it, if the dream is accurate."

Dr. Lledrith stood and refilled all their wine glasses nearly to the brim, but remained silent. Her lips were firmly pinched together, as if she fought with herself to say more.

Jack took this as a sign that things were worse than his half-remembered dream indicated. He reached for his glass and drank half down. "Something happened, didn't it?"

Aneurin's face was beet red. He kept shooting pleading glances at both Jack and Dr. Lledrith. "Yes. We'd both forgotten by then that you'd been abused. When I entered you, the memory surfaced. You went mad, I would say, screaming about the darkness and pain. You begged me for your freedom." He shuddered and his eyes filled with tears. "It was heart wrenching to hear."

Jack held up his hand to forestall Dr. Lledrith drawing breath for a clinical analysis. "No need to say more. I can well guess. Add to that your guilt about making love with someone so young, even if technically you were the same age, and your guilt made you do something foolish?"

Aneurin bowed his head. "By then, I was older, Jack. While you were at school, I'd go back in time and age myself. I'd been doing it for years, because dragons age so slowly. By that day, I was fully in my prime, equal to the age you are now, I'd say. I should have known better than to touch a boy."

"But I wasn't a boy anymore, by human laws, Aneurin. I was eighteen."

Dr. Lledrith shrugged, her voice heavy with disapproval. "Not really. Your true birthday was a few weeks later. That's not the point. What Aneurin did about your trauma was much more a crime."

Jack looked down to where their hands remained locked. He made his voice soft and loving. No matter how stunning all this was, Aneurin was not guilty of any crime. In fact, if anyone was guilty, it was Jack. He'd left his dragon because of a memory. Now Jack felt like a first class heel. "Was that the so-called ill-conceived spell?"

Nodding, Aneurin broke their contact and took a gulp of wine. "I broke our laws, Jack. Without your consent, I altered your mind and erased your memory of me, our times together, everything. For all intents, I ceased to exist for you."

Jack stood, clenching his wine glass until the stem shattered. Part of him was grateful for the absolution of guilt, and part of him didn't get it. The latter won, and spoke the question his heart screamed. "Why, Aneurin? Why? You were probably the one thing about my childhood that was pure love and innocent fun. Everything else was dutiful obedience in a drab world."

Aneurin stood, his golden eyes full of tears that fell unheeded down his sculpted cheeks. "I wasn't thinking. I just wanted your pain to end, and I believed I'd caused your distress. I thought it best if you didn't remember me at all."

Jack picked up his old shirt and wiped his hands. Thankfully, he'd not cut himself. "Your spell didn't work well. You gave me many nights of dreams."

Dr. Lledrith cut in. "More than that, Jack. He cut himself off from you. A soul-bonded dragon without their human half weakens and dies. If you hadn't dreamt of him, and fed him your life energy, he would have been a pile of bones by now. That's how we live, attached to a human."

Aneurin paced away from them both and stood facing the fireplace with his back to them. "I wanted to die, and wondered why I couldn't."

Dr. Lledrith slammed her wine glass on the table and shoved back her chair.

Jack quelled Dr. Lledrith with a look. He understood her anger, but this was for him to solve. He walked over to Aneurin and took the larger man in his arms. "Sorry, lover dragon, but you're not allowed. You and I have been like cuckoo's eggs."

Aneurin's body remained stiff as a board. "What's a cuckoo?"

"A bird that lays its egg in another bird's nest and the young are raised by a foster mother bird of another species." He stroked Aneurin's silky black hair, still marveling at the length. "Our mothers couldn't raise us, so we survived on our own with only each other for company. Sorry, dragon. You're stuck with your human."

Aneurin relaxed in his arms. "You forgive me so easily for hurting you?"

Jack motioned behind his back, shooing Dr. Lledrith away. A small popping sound of displaced air told him she was gone. "You took care of me when I was unable. Now it's my turn. You're still blind as a bat."

A snort of warm air teased Jack's skin on his neck. "Bats see fine. I know, I had a few stay with me."

Jack snuck a glance over his shoulder. Yes, Dr. Lledrith was gone. "It's an expression. Just like cuckoo's egg. We need a new expression for us, though." He thought for a moment. "Dragon's eggs. Left to fend for ourselves, we took care of each other instead of being cared for by others. Once we get your eyes fixed, we have a mission to fulfill."

Aneurin lifted his head in alarm. "We can't fix my eyes, Jack. If I go unconscious, I'll revert to my reptilian form."

Jack still had hold of Aneurin's shoulders. He shook them slightly. "This time you'll have to trust human magic. There's something called laser surgery. You are awake during the whole thing. It's like --" He searched for a way to explain lasers."-- like a light shining in your eye."

Aneurin's chin went up. "That doesn't sound so bad. Then what mission will we go on?"

Jack grinned. "I'm mage born, right? So, I need to learn magic. You promised to teach me to fly. Then, we're going to go find my -- Cadell."

"Why in the name of my foremothers would we do that?" Aneurin's horror at such a suggestion was clear.

"The dragon's eggs have hatched. Our mothers have put themselves in harm's way all these years, acting as bait to Cadell's revenge, to protect us. Time for a little payback."

Aneurin laughed. "That suits me very well indeed!" He sobered. "That means going to America, and dressing like you do. Will I have to wear the little string too?"

Jack chuckled. "Thong, Aneurin. Thong. No, you don't have to wear one of those. In fact, I fully intend to keep my dragon naked a great deal of the time." He paused and smiled. "There's more to this than just revenge, though, Aneurin. My memory is full of holes. I'm going to need your help to sort them out. When you're not teaching me magic and mayhem, that is."

Aneurin chuckled and nibbled on his neck. "I think we can combine a few of those activities."

"That sounds good to me." Jack laid his head on Aneurin's shoulder. Whoever, whatever, he was, they'd deal with it. The important thing was, he'd never be without his dragon again.

Dragon's Stone
Lena Austin

Jack has more problems than you can shake a wand at. He's the son of the usurper to the throne, an untrained wizard with a powerful gift, a gay dragonrider, and a cryptozoologist in a world full of mythical creatures.

Now he's going to school where one of his teachers is a biker turned dragonrider. Men are treated as second-class citizens in Honalee, so this is his one chance to be something other than a stud wizard for the local sorceresses. If that wasn't bad enough, some mythical object called the Dragon's Stone has been stolen. How much do they expect of a reluctant heir to the throne, anyway?

Chapter One

It was a dark and stormy night…

Jack turned away from the window in disgust. Now he was thinking in clichés. Wasn't his life crazier than any novelist could dream up? Okay, so the thunderstorms had lasted four days already, cooping him in the apartment with his lover, Aneurin. Normally, this would not be a bad prospect. Normally being the operative word. Nothing in his life would ever be normal again. Not when his lover was a dragon and he was a wizard in the modern day Washington, DC area.

Aneurin's sleeping dragon form took up a large portion of Jack's generous penthouse living room. The large napping sofa Jack had previously owned hadn't lasted past the first time Aneurin took his pain pills. After the eye surgery to correct his cataracts two days ago, he'd needed them. Where one pain-wracked man had sat, a dragon lounged in rubble.

Jack shrugged, and a grin crept over his face. His heart lightened. Oh, well. What was the value of mere stuff when you had love? He crept over to lovingly rub his dragon's scaly muzzle.

Aneurin's contented sigh ruffled Jack's hair, and the gold-tipped tail ceased its restless movement.

Jack reached up and adjusted the blue silk bed sheet now serving as a draconic blindfold. They'd given up trying to keep Aneurin in human form when the pain pills made him so stoned he'd revert to his reptilian form as soon as he fell asleep.

Aneurin's voice crept softly into his head, still slurred with sleep and narcotic. "J-Jack? Is it Wednesday yet?"

His heart wrenching a little, Jack kissed the purple muzzle. "No, not quite. It's Tuesday evening.

Tomorrow we take your bandages off, lover dragon. We'll have a lovely time in the shower, washing away all that goo the doctor put on your eyes, and then you'll be able to see again. Tonight, you'll probably need just a mild analgesic instead of those little pills that make you sleep."

A draconic purr rumbled. "Good. I'm tired of sleeping all the time. I smell rain, though." The gigantic head sank slowly down to rest on his forepaws. "Guess we'll have to wait on your flying lessons again. Can't wait to go home and get a proper riding saddle for my aching back, anyway. You've got a bony ass."

Jack chuckled and hid his lurch of fear. He patted Aneurin's soft nose comfortingly. He didn't want to go to Honalee. Not yet. Ironically, all those years he'd thought himself an orphan, he'd dreamt of his parents. Now he practically quaked in terror at the thought of making the dimensional leap and meeting his mother at last. "Liar. My weight is insignificant, and my bony ass sits between two of your ridge scales. I'm the one with his balls divided by a hard plate of dragon hide, and I'm the one who about froze to death in that cold mountain air."

The trip to the Rockies and a secluded mountain cabin while they waited for Aneurin's turn on the operating table had not gone well. Without anything to protect his privates from hard dragon spinal ridges, the first leap in the air had been painful and the situation hadn't improved. He also hadn't been able to change form. His magic was still very shaky and weak. The results had been messy. He'd managed to get as far as a very misshapen semi-humanoid form with scales and wings, and it had taken them hours to get the wings off his back and make him appear human again.

Snuggling again into his pillows, Aneurin mumbled something about "low ambient magic levels" and began to snore.

Jack stepped gingerly over the pile of blankets that made up Aneurin's improvised bed and went back to his dining room table where his laptop hummed patiently. The spreadsheet detailing the sales of all his investment properties seemed like his execution orders. All his wealth now resided in safe bonds, T-notes, and CDs, locked in several banks under the watchful supervision of lawyers and accountants who eyed each other with suspicion. The sales were complete. Only this penthouse remained as his one property. Everything was in order for him to leave for Honalee.

He slugged down the cold remains of his coffee and strode toward the kitchen to brew a fresh pot. He was going to miss coffee in Honalee, but without one bit of electricity, there would be no way he could take his beloved professional coffeemaker with all the gadgets a coffee snob could want.

Lucynda's latest letter, written in her perfect calligraphy, lay like a recrimination beside the stove. He'd memorized the words her dragon, Draig, had read to him. He estimated the note was written at about the level of third grade in the language of Honalee, but his mother's dragon had been very pleased. He'd almost forgiven Draig for her deception at pretending to be his therapist.

Guilt twisted knife-sharp in his guts at the memory of her loving attempt to understand why he hadn't just hopped on Aneurin's back and come to her immediately once he'd known of her existence. "I don't understand half of what Draig tells me, son, but if you need to do these things before you can come for a visit,

I must agree. What are a few more months after nearly thirty years? I will wait. With much love, Lucynda."

Jack rubbed his aching forehead and put the letter back down. How could this woman he didn't remember love him so? After being an orphan all his life, having a mother seemed impossible. He wanted to know her. He did. Yet he was so terrified of the prospect.

A warm hand covered his.

He gasped and snatched his hand back. His body straightened.

Draig's sympathetic blue eyes gazed back at him. His mother's dragon stood in her human form, in her guise of the therapist Dr. Lledrith. "I teleported in to check on Aneurin. Still zoned on codeine, isn't he?"

Jack jerked his chin in what might be interpreted as a nod. Embarrassment at being caught in an emotional state by his former therapist and also Aneurin's mother made him blush. If he didn't look at her, maybe her sharp eyes wouldn't catch on to his torn emotions. He turned to get Draig her coffee. He put the largest bottle of honey he could buy beside the mug and rummaged for a spoon. "Yeah, he's going to still be a bit stoned for the next couple of hours. He'll be on Tylenol tonight, though."

She poured an obscene amount of honey into a large mug and then added coffee and cream. "Good. We can talk about you in relative peace then. Come on, Jack. You need a sympathetic ear right now." Her heels clicked on his dining room floor before she planted herself in a chair at the table and shoved aside his laptop.

Damn. He knew he was in for a lecture now. Draig would show him no mercy, pitilessly analyzing his psyche and laying his neuroses all out like bones to dry in the sun. "Draig, I…"

She snorted, but her eyes twinkled warmly. "You need a friend, not your therapist. Since my son is presently unfit to provide a shoulder --" Her gaze flicked for a moment to Aneurin when he snored hard enough to blow over a potted palm. "-- I'll just have to do. Besides, I have a message for you."

Jack's hands shook slightly while he poured a fresh mug of aromatic brew. He breathed in the scent to lock it in his memory, knowing he deliberately delayed hearing another plea from Lucynda. Maybe if he called her that, if they didn't like each other, the disappointment wouldn't hurt so much. *Coward.* Jack tried for cocky and nonchalant. "Yeah? How's Mother doing?"

His mother's lover and dragon wrapped her hands around her honey laced with a little coffee. Dragons had such a sweet tooth for the sticky stuff. "Lucynda is fine. This message doesn't come from her. I'm sorry to say this comes from the royal council. You've been discovered, Jack. Somehow."

He cocked his head to one side and sat down on the opposite side of the table. Her words were ominous, but he didn't get the problem. "Hey, don't make it sound like I've committed a crime or something. So the royal council knows Lucynda the Red Sorceress has a son. Big deal."

"Actually, this is a big deal." She sipped her coffee. "Honalee doesn't have many male wizards." She drew a parchment scroll out of her purse. "Jack, son of the Red Sorceress, you have been invited to be tested and trained at the Royal Academy for Wizards." She tossed the scroll across the table with an air of contempt.

Jack's brows drew together into a puzzled frown. The fancy red seal, laced with little gold flecks, sparkled even in the light of the chandelier. The ink smelled funny now that he'd quit smoking and had a nose again. Something about that parchment made him nervous enough to want a cigarette. On the other hand, perhaps it was the way Draig seemed to treat this like a punishment. "Why do I get the feeling you don't approve of this?"

"I don't." She bit the words off like they were a bit of meat she chomped. "I'd rather Lucynda trained you, since you're too old to foster to another wizard. Your bond with Aneurin is strong enough to not need further improvement. You proved that by communicating with each other over a vast ocean, even if you did it in dreams. Flying is nothing, once you have the proper equipment. The rest can be taught by any competent mage, male or female. Special academy for males. Pah!" A tiny puff of flame spit briefly out of her mouth, emphasizing her contempt.

Jack jerked back from the sulfurous stench of dragon breath, not out of any real fear. He'd never seen fire appear out of a dragon's human form before, and his internal cryptozoologist made a note of the phenomenon. He'd have burned his lips.

Jack was of two minds on this academy thing. First, at thirty-two, he felt a little old to go to school. He had visions of sitting in some sort of dungeon classroom surrounded by teenagers, waving a wand and learning to levitate feathers in pidgin Latin. Not his idea of good time. Then again, he'd really enjoyed college and did well in a structured learning environment. "Aren't I a little old to be going to school?"

She snorted. "In my opinion, yes. Nevertheless, there it is. Consider the invitation a royal command." She drank the rest of her coffee in one gulp and stood. "Your mentor might show up to give you the details. Be nice to her. She comes from the king of humans. I suggest you stop procrastinating and get to Honalee. You'll want a few days to acclimate and shop for your supplies. You certainly can't do without a wand, and a dragon saddle would be wise before you unman yourself." She grinned. "Lucynda is looking forward to shopping in the village. She's already ordered a seamstress to make robes for you."

Stunned, Jack blurted the first thing that popped into his head. "Robes? I am not wearing a fucking dress!"

Draig stared, then laughed. "It's not a dress. Oh, this is going to be so amusing. I can't wait to see what Honalee makes of you!" She popped out of sight.

Rubbing his aching head, Jack stomped back into the kitchen for more brew. "Oh, that makes me want to go, definitely. I don't care what you say. It's a dress. Bad enough I have to do without coffee, electricity, email, and money."

"So take instant coffee, twit, and wear jeans underneath your robes."

Aneurin's voice in his head startled Jack enough to make him miss the cup as he poured. He grabbed a handful of paper towels to mop up the mess. Blech. Instant? Well, the fake coffee would be better than doing without. "Good points, carrion breath. How are you feeling?"

Aneurin raised his purple head from his forelegs. "Better. My eyes feel glued shut, but they don't hurt much now. Sorry I didn't defend you a little while my mother was here. I didn't feel like being cooed over like a hatchling."

Jack had to tease his friend. He pranced over and purred in the most syrupy voice he could manage. "How's my darling Aneurin? Feeling better? Let me adjust your bandages. Want me to spoon feed you some honey, my sweet love?"

Aneurin's tail whipped out and knocked Jack on his ass into the blankets. "Don't make me ill."

Jack laughed so hard he couldn't have dodged anyway. "Aww, no honey?"

One claw raked his clothes, shredding them to rags. Third set that month, gone. The open jar of honey floated from the kitchen and tipped over on him, covering Jack from neck to knees in a thin stream. Aneurin's forked tongue followed the stream, rasping like a cat's. "Don't mind if I do. The smell of the open jar was driving me to distraction."

Jack gasped. Dragon tongue on his body turned him on, and Aneurin knew this. Jack's cock twitched to life. It had been days since they'd made love, and he was hornier than a three-peckered billy goat. "How'd you know where to pour?"

Aneurin snickered and changed to naked human, falling on Jack to lick with a more human tongue, even if it was still slightly forked. The blanket that had been his mask changed into a neat blue bandage around his eyes only. "I'm still reptilian. My tongue tastes the air, my nose smells the scents, and I get a picture of sorts. Not as good as my eyes, but these other senses do the job. Now shut up. I want a snack of honey and my human's flesh." He attacked Jack's cock like a hungry dog went after a tasty bone.

His human shut up. Aneurin's teeth were sharp enough to enforce the command. Not that Jack minded.

If his lover felt up to a little horizontal tango, then he was willing to go along. Short of a shower, a dragon tongue bath sounded like an excellent notion. "I'm not going to complain. You suck cock like a pro."

The dragon didn't bother to lift his head from swallowing all Jack's meat, just asked telepathically, "A pro what?"

Momentarily distracted by Aneurin's finger sliding toward his anus, Jack moaned. He should have known he'd have to explain. "A person who sells sexual favors for money."

Aneurin stopped to consider this. "Oh. Well, I suppose one who does this for a career would be very good. I'm complimented." His finger tickled, then slid in gently.

Jack gritted his teeth against the heat flooding his groin. His head whirled, probably from the lack of blood to his brain. "If you keep that up, I'm not going to last long."

Aneurin paused, and lifted his head. "Well, that might be a problem. Tell me what you see in this room. I heard clinking and splashing."

Jack turned his head and gasped. Every loose object in the room that weighed less than five pounds floated in some weird waltz above their heads. His favorite coffee cup was doing a dance with a vase of silk flowers. Jack's prized laptop bobbed along near the ceiling next to some books. Then everything all came crashing down on their heads.

* * *

Aneurin instinctively covered Jack's body with his own as soon as he heard the first impact of smashing glass and the low grunt from Jack. Crashes of metal and shattering dishes made it seem like the whole apartment tumbled from the sky. He shifted to dragon form, resolved to rip off the bandages and carry Jack away despite the consequences if he felt one shake of the floor beneath him.

Protected by Aneurin's head, Jack ceased movement and waited for the rain of destruction to stop. He muttered under his breath, but Aneurin heard his mind easily. After a stream of inventive word combinations Aneurin had learned were curses, Jack settled into orderly thoughts. "I thought you said there was low ambient magic here. Shit, Aneurin, you should see this mess." One last impact and tinkle emphasized his words.

Aneurin kept to dragon form, where he felt strongest. Despite the anxiety in Jack's voice, Aneurin detected no real fear or pain. Jack was all right, so he could relax somewhat. "What happened?"

A high-pitched female voice answered in the tongue of Honalee. "It appears Jack can levitate objects without the assist of a wand."

Jack scrambled to cover his body with a blanket and rested against Aneurin's scaly chest. Points for Jack -- he managed relative calm. "No shit, Sherlock. Who are you? And doesn't anyone from Honalee know the meaning of knocking?"

Aneurin's other senses showed him a human female shape standing near the doorway. She did not move, or seem threatening in any way, but he snarled just in case. Jack was nearly naked and between his foreclaws. A dragon would be his defense. If she made one move to harm him, Aneurin would dine on human for lunch and worry about getting the taste out of his mouth later.

The sorceress, for she could be nothing less to have arrived here without a dragon, sniffed contemptuously in the snarling dragon's direction.

"Oh, do stop that, dragon. I do not intend to harm your bonded." She glided forward, clearly a lady of the human court, for they insisted ladies took only tiny steps instead of striding forth confidently. He remembered his mother telling him stories of Lucynda's deportment lessons when they were young.

Aneurin took an instant dislike to her -- to be called "dragon" as if he were unintelligent was highly insulting -- and couldn't stop the hiss in his throat. He was surprised to smell a hint of blood on her. How odd. The hiss died unuttered. Blood? Fresh blood? On a lady who probably entered the kitchens of her castle but three times a year?

Jack stood, moving from under Aneurin's muzzle until he stood erect. He laid his hand casually on the dragon's cheek and gave his lover dragon a pat. "My dragon has a name, ma'am. It's Aneurin. Since you already know mine, the courtesy of an introduction might be the next order of business." His Honalean was full of mispronunciations, but clear enough.

Judging by the heat flare Aneurin sensed around the woman's face, he assumed she blushed beet red at Jack's naked state. Jack had not bothered to bring the blanket with him. The bright color belied her tart response. "The first order of business for you is clothing, if you please."

Aneurin swallowed a snicker, since he could easily read Jack's annoyance at her intrusion. He'd shredded Jack's clothes, so he probably stood there wearing nothing but his shoes and a smile of pure mischief.

Jack snorted and turned toward his bedroom, kicking debris out of his way as he went. "Next time, knock and you won't catch someone *in flagrante delicto*." He sauntered into the room, and Aneurin heard his closet door open.

The sorceress seemed nonplussed for a moment. "What do those words mean?"

The amused dragon answered. "He meant, if you knock first, you wouldn't catch someone fucking."

Jack called from the bedroom. "Yeah, we're gay. So lose the seductive pink dress, willya? I could care less what your tits look like."

Her gulp was clearly audible. "Oh." She stood silently for a moment. "We appear to have gotten off on the wrong footing. We shall start over. My name is Lady Tilda, and I'm sorry to have caused offense. I'll knock next time, but I shan't change my dress. It's the king's favorite."

Aneurin started using his tail to sweep the mess into one pile as a distraction to keep from laughing. Jack's cocky attitude kept Lady Tilda off balance, and Aneurin wasn't about to disturb his little play. Jack sent him an image of what this female looked like to human eyes, and Aneurin was forced to mask his laughter with a fit of coughing. He buried his nose in his blanket nest in case he coughed up a bit of gas and set it alight. The pink dress she wore made the blue-eyed blonde resemble a confection Jack had purchased for him called a cupcake. He'd been ready to defend Jack from that?

Jack came back into the room, and even through the blankets, his draconic nose could smell the leather. Two could play the game of keeping the other off balance by wearing seductive clothing. He was unaffected by her costume, but she liked males, that much was obvious. No doubt Jack wore the full outfit he knew Aneurin loved -- black leather pants, black silk shirt, and a long, black leather vest that swept around his booted ankles. Jack knew what that outfit did to Aneurin's cock, which hardened even at the thought.

From Lady Tilda's intake of breath, and the heat that suffused her whole body, Aneurin hazarded Jack's ploy had worked. She cleared her throat noisily and turned her head. "Excuse me. I'm unused to the way men dress here."

Aneurin kept his nose in the blankets. He could hear Jack's wicked response of, "Good. Two can play your sexual game," in his mind. Aneurin warned Jack to back off or he'd set the blankets on fire choking back laughter.

His voice was mild and courteous. "I'm sorry to cause offense." He paused and let his echo of her words sink in. "I assume you are the mentor I was told would be forthcoming? May I offer you a chair and a beverage, if I can find an unbroken glass?"

Her naturally high-pitched voice lowered from a squeak to something less painful. "Yes to all questions. Wine, if you have it."

"Let's see what I can salvage." His boots rang on the hardwood, and then on the tile in the kitchen. "It appears nothing was damaged in the cabinets. Ah, and I have some chilled champagne in the fridge."

She sat in a chair at the table, choosing the one to the right of the traditional head of the table. Aneurin found that interesting. She was used to authority positions, despite her ornamental appearance. "That would be excellent. I've never had chilled wine before. Let's start with what I intended to say, despite our inauspicious beginning. I see you do belong in the Royal Academy. You must get your magic under control, Lord Jack. You cannot permit such activity every time you have sex with your dragon. I can see why the Red Sorceress is sponsoring you."

"Spons… Really? Interesting." Jack brought back the glasses and handed one to Lady Tilda. "Why do you call me Lord?"

Her tinkling giggle might appeal to the king, but it made Aneurin nauseated. "Oh, the bubbles tickle. Why, you're Lucynda's sister's son, aren't you? That makes you son of the Duchess of Harringdon, and a Lord. I'm sorry your mother felt it necessary to hide you in this non-magical world to protect you from her enemies. Rather drastic if you ask me, but no one did. Lucynda did tell me you were ignorant of Honalee, having lived here all your life."

She waved away Jack's answer. "No, don't worry your head about it. We'll soon have you all prepared to be a fine wizard, and that's much better than being a noble consort, isn't it? I'll expect you at the Academy testing in a fortnight. Do try to acquire proper clothing by then. Tah!" She popped out of sight before Jack could draw breath.

Aneurin groaned and burrowed deeper in the blankets. Now he was in trouble. He'd forgotten that one aspect of human culture in Honalee. Jack wasn't going to like this one bit. He counted three heartbeats until Jack exploded.

"Patronizing bitch! What the fuck was all that about? Why am I suddenly the son of some duchess instead of Lucynda?" Jack paced around the room, so full of anger Aneurin could see magic vibrating objects around him, even without his eyes. Then he stopped dead in his tracks. "Oh, I get it. They can't let word get out that Lucynda's son has returned so my fath… Cadell can't find me. At least not until I get this weird-ass telekinesis of mine under control. I probably light up magically like a neon sign. Fine. I can see the necessity." He blew out a breath. "A fortnight? What is that in terms I can understand?"

His lover breathed a little easier. Aneurin did not want to explain why Lady Tilda spoke to Jack like he was a lesser being. Jack would find out soon enough, and Aneurin preferred his wrath focused on someone else when he did. "A fortnight is fourteen days, Jack."

His poor human wizard started like he'd been zapped by a mage bolt. "Oh, shit and shinola. I'd better go pack. Looks like we're leaving for Honalee in the morning. I'll be damned if I am rude enough to say, 'Hi Mom. Nice to meet you. I'm leaving for this dimwitted school tomorrow. Nice knowing you!' Even if we hate each other, I can always come back here to wait, right?"

Chapter Two

Jack pulled the ropes tight, hopefully securing his luggage to Aneurin's back. They'd improvised a pad of sorts to protect his family jewels between Aneurin's spine ridges. He jumped down from the coffee table he'd used as an improvised ladder. "If my Samsonite can survive baggage handlers at the airports, I think it can weather a dimensional flight. How's that feel, pal?"

Aneurin tore his eyes away from the windows. Since the bandage had come off, he relished every view he could get, and Jack didn't begrudge keeping the large window curtains open for a panoramic display to please his friend's newly regained sight. A draconic shake rattled every one of the bags strapped to his body. "They seem secure. Hurry, Jack. It's late afternoon in Honalee. We're expected for dinner, and you'll want time to unpack."

Jack shrugged on his leather overcoat and pulled on gloves. He took one last look at the sprawl of Washington, DC sparkling like some giant's spilled treasure in the pre-dawn darkness. Traffic would soon clog the beltway, and the noise of the ever-present mass of humanity would rise to deafening levels. Yet, it was what he knew. Could he really live without his cell phone, PDA, computer, and coffee in exchange for learning about all the creatures of myth and legend? Hell, he could try. No one said he couldn't come back and patronize a Starbucks if he got desperate. Jack used the coffee table one last time to climb up, and wrapped one rope securely across his thighs as a seatbelt of sorts. Feeling a little like a Blues Brother, he put on a pair of wraparound sunglasses and snapped the elastic around his head. "Okay, Aneurin. Let's get this show on the road."

Damn dragon must have been afraid he'd change his mind, because he wasted no time. He unfurled his wings as much as he could. "Hang tight. This may be uncomfortable."

"Now he tells me!"

The darkness of his apartment was replaced for an instant with pure black nothingness. Jack's stomach lurched. Then his eyes were blinded by afternoon sunlight, even with his sunglasses. Hey, they were falling. Shit, they were plummeting.

Aneurin's wings snapped out fully and caught the wind. Jack's guts were left behind, and they soared effortlessly high above the green valley below. Beneath him, Jack felt Aneurin's bones stretch until they popped audibly. "Ahh! I needed that," the dragon sighed gustily. "There's a thermal ahead. We'll use it to circle around until we find the castle with a red roof, just as Draig told us."

Even Jack felt the difference in the temperature when the dragon found the uplifting column of warm air, and they took a fast invisible elevator skyward. Jack whooped, beginning to enjoy himself. So what if he was getting windburn already? The view was spectacular, and the whole place shimmered with green. A village below looked so perfect he wanted a camera before he remembered there'd be no digital processing. He hung on to the ropes and tried to spot a castle with a red roof somewhere in the south of Honalee.

Aneurin roared, nearly deafening him. "There it is!"

Weren't wizards' castles supposed to be gray stone edifices lodged into the sides of craggy mountains? Instead, Lucynda's castle was a whitewashed or limestone home easily the size of a mansion, with a collection of smaller buildings nestled around it, like chicks around a mother hen. It looked a little like Neuschwanstein. No real fancy flower gardens, just small farm plots of maybe a half acre each, though the wide footpaths in between looked paved with cobblestones or something. Neat and orderly. He liked it. "Nice place!"

One of the larger buildings Jack thought was a barn more closely resembled an aircraft hangar. He laughed and pointed. "Hey, Aneurin! If that's not a dragon abode, I'll eat my boots!"

"Your boots are in no danger. There's Draig."

Sure enough, a lavender and silver dragon stepped out of the dragon hangar, unfurled her wings, and roared before leaping into the sky. She joined them in an aerial bout of soaring and aerobatics. "It's about time you got here! Welcome home!"

Jack clutched tightly to the ropes and hung on for his life while Aneurin and his mother apparently did what dragons do when they met in the air as friends -- fly their tails off. What the hell -- let them have their fun. He protested only when he felt the improvised saddle beneath him start to slip to one side. "Hey! Cut that out, you two! Remember there's a human held on only by ropes up here!"

Contritely, they both backwinged to land. No blanket could protect him from the jarring his nuts took from the impact. He groaned and bent over as soon as they were safely on the ground. Breathing hurt.

Aneurin snaked his head around. "Sorry about that. We'll get a saddle tomorrow, I promise. Get off and jump around until they settle. I'll kiss them in apology later." His nose whuffled at him and nudged.

Jack sat proudly up, determined to look semi-intelligent when he met his mother. Crossed eyes and moans of pain weren't going to help his image. He swung one leg over and slid down Aneurin's side until he hit the ground, barely containing his nausea. He hoped he hadn't turned white. At least he managed to stay upright, despite the agonizing state of his balls.

Dignity, man, dignity. Jack discreetly did a few hops in place until his nuts decided it was safe to come out. He could live with the throbbing. He hoped. "I might let you, if the jewels aren't the size of grapefruits by nightfall. Yeah, let's get a saddle tomorrow, first thing."

Draig stepped around Aneurin's tail, furling her wings into place. "Nice suit, Jack. Not a bad compromise on what's closest to medieval garb without your feeling silly until you're used to it. By the way, speaking of leather, there's a leather worker in the village. DeAngelo should have a few saddles made, since he has royal patronage. He'll tool something lovely for you." Her eyes, still the same bright blue as they were in her human form, looked at something over his shoulder. "Oh, good. Here comes Lucynda."

Jack swallowed and fought down nerves. Worse, he desperately wanted a cigarette. One deep breath, and Jack did his best about face to meet the woman he'd thought for thirty years had abandoned him. Would he have the guts to say the words he'd rehearsed endlessly?

* * *

Jack eyed the woman who hauled her skirts in a wad and made an undignified run down the steps. Brown hair, blue eyes. Younger looking than he'd expected, considering she had to be around fifty. Somewhere in there. Still, there was something comfortable about her. Maybe it was the laugh lines and the twinkle in her eyes. It didn't matter. He liked her, and that was enough for now.

She halted a few feet away from him and planted her fists on her hips. She studied him from the tips of his boots to the top of his head, craning her neck since the top of her head barely cleared his chest. "Well! The other world hasn't been overfeeding you, have they? We'll fix that. Welcome home, son. Draig tells me you're used to being called Jack."

"Yes, ma'am. Um. Hi, Mom. I'm home?" Jack's brain plagued him with images of a TV character shouting "Lucy! I'm home!" "Maybe over dinner you can tell me what my birth name was?"

The tiny sorceress' lips twitched, then she laughed. "Overwhelmed, aren't you? I do apologize. Let's get Aneurin settled, and then we'll let you unpack. Unless you'd prefer he slept with you?"

Jack blinked for a moment. His gaze flickered to the big wood and stone hangar structure. He guessed it was normal for a dragon to sleep in the hangar, or whatever it was called. Who knew? Aneurin might want to spend time with his own mother. Jack swallowed a childish need to cling to the one constant in all this and turned to Aneurin. "It's up to you, lover. What's your pleasure?"

Aneurin shifted to his human form and paced forward to caress Jack's jaw. "As if I'd leave you alone here. I promised, didn't I?" He brushed a quick kiss on Jack's lips.

Clearing his throat, Jack felt heat rush into his face like some fucking girl caught necking. Was getting a public kiss from your lover acceptable in Honalee? He stole a guilty glance at Lucynda and then breathed a sigh of relief. "Thanks, pal."

Draig had also changed form, and now cuddled her human in her arms. "See? Nothing to worry about, now, is there?"

Lucynda peeked at Jack, her eyes bright with unshed tears. She smiled tremulously at him, and her face was redder than his.

Jack's eyes widened. It took no brains to figure out Draig had told Lucynda of his anger and bitterness at his orphaned state, and now Lucynda had reason to fear he'd hate her. He cleared his throat. "I seem to remember some injudicious statements made about my parents before I found out I wasn't really an abandoned orphan." He paused and searched for words. "Nice to know I'm not, and I was wrong."

Hope shimmered in her eyes. "M... Jack... I..." She faltered and couldn't seem to go on.

He threw back his shoulders and steeled himself. This next step took more courage than he ever thought he had. He opened his arms. "Can I have a hug?"

Now her tears fell, but they were overshadowed by a glittering smile. Step by hesitant step, she left Draig's arms until she leapt the last two feet into his arms, sobbing. "Thank you! Thank you!"

Had he been overwhelmed before? The feelings in his chest threatened to choke him now. He coughed and held tight. *Say something, dummy. Anything.* "You know, I kind of figured you'd be a lot bigger."

She sniffled. "Is that so? Well, I remember you being a lot smaller. Funny how the mind plays tricks upon you, isn't it?" She wriggled out of his arms and smoothed her gown. Then she waved over two menservants. "I'll let you compose yourself and we'll meet for a simple feast in the great hall. I'm sorry it's so little. Only seven courses."

Because you really didn't believe I'd come, did you? Well, he didn't blame her for her doubts. Hadn't he been filled with uncertainty? "Sure, seven courses are fine." He'd have been happy with a pizza, but she didn't need to know that.

Jack followed his mother up the lawn and into his new home, with Aneurin's hand clasped in his.

* * *

Aneurin reluctantly allowed Jack to drag him from shop to shop in the wizard's village. The merchandise required by the school barely interested Jack, and he usually purchased whatever the shopkeeper said was good with no bargaining. Aneurin shook his head and tried another admonishment. "Jack, you really ought to shop more carefully. Don't you care about your wand, scales, cauldron and herbs? You could have been sold sticks, grass and leaves for all you know."

Jack stepped happily down off the modest stoop of the herb shop, his interested gaze darting around at all the shoppers clogging the dirt lane. He pulled Aneurin over to the side so a dwarf, so laden with packages you couldn't see his beard, could enter the shop. Jack courteously opened the door for the burdened fellow, and then closed the door after the astonished dwarf entered. "That's the point, old pal. I haven't a clue what I'm doing, and no way to know differently. Oh, wow! Look, Aneurin. Is that an Elf? Wow, they really are graceful, aren't they? Hey, is that a troll?"

Aneurin grabbed the back of Jack's leather trench coat before Jack could go charging over to talk to another "mythical being." Poor Lucynda had conceded the trench was the closest thing to the robes denoting a wizard Jack possessed and had reluctantly allowed him to wear it for the shopping excursion. "Jack, stop. You've accosted a werewolf already. Let's go buy my saddle before you indulge in any more conversations. I'm getting thirsty."

Jack laughed and shrugged, completely unrepentant. "Sorry, Aneurin. I don't mean to embarrass you. All right, where do we buy dragon saddles?"

Sighing, Aneurin shifted the basket containing their purchases and pointed to a sign that read *Fyne Leather and Saddlery*. "There, the big barn-like structure with the red shutters. Just try to keep in mind you're the son of a duchess. A little dignity, please?"

With a grimace, Jack nodded his agreement. "Bad enough my birth name was Mikalus. You're beginning to sound like Mother. That long tedious explanation over dinner about her sister's status was enough to put me off that excellent food, even if I did freak to see a whole pig presented on the table. That was a little meal? I don't want to know what a feast is like, then." He opened the door to the shop and pushed Aneurin in first. "I'll be a good little student wizard, I promise."

That whispered comment didn't reassure Aneurin much. Jack had no concept of rank or class distinctions. To him, the whole world was his equal, even other races. To Aneurin, this was a point in Jack's favor, but the rigid social structure of Honalee would likely be less tolerant.

His lover happily crossed the street and marched up to a man sitting on a stool outside the huge red doors of the barn, his feet propped up on a barrel. Grizzled gray hair straggled out from what Aneurin would have called the oddest hat he'd ever seen to form a ponytail down the wizard's back. Only wizards had long hair in Honalee. The old man curiously studied Jack from the tips of his sneakers to the top of his head.

Jack grinned and nodded. "Hey, nice Stetson! Are you the owner of this place? I need a saddle, please."

The old wizard frowned at Jack's pronunciations of Honalean words. His thumb flicked his hat a trifle higher. "Nice set of Nikes. Why don't you try speaking English, Jack?"

Aneurin dropped the basket and his jaw simultaneously. The old wizard spoke perfect American English.

Breathing a gusty sigh of relief, Jack stuck out his hand. "Oh, man, someone who speaks my language! Wonderful. How'd you know my name? What's yours, by the way?"

Grinning, the wizard clasped Jack's hand and they moved their arms up and down in unison. "My name's DeAngelo, and I'll be your dragon riding instructor at the school. That's how I know about you. Come on in and meet my dragon, Watash. We'll have a beer." He kicked his feet off the barrel and stood, a short stocky man in a simple tunic and trews. Only his hat was oddly out of place in the world of Honalee.

Aneurin sheepishly picked up his basket and spent a moment gathering up the spilled contents from the hard packed soil. Relief flooded him. He knew Watash, and hoped he might have a few minutes with the old dragon for news of dragonkind his mother hadn't provided.

Jack moaned and licked his lips. "Beer? American or British? I'd kill for a beer, or better yet, coffee."

DeAngelo chuckled. "I was born in Michigan to a rebel wizard and his non-mage wife. Good cold American Michelob. Sorry, I polished off the last of my coffee this morning. I have to brew it in a camp stove percolator, so I don't keep much around. Watash and I will go back to Seattle and pick up a pound or two before school starts. Want me to grab you some, too?" He shoved open the barn door wide enough to admit them. "I'll pick up another percolator while I'm at it. You'll be able to brew a pot for yourself at the fire in your room at school. Better than that watered down piss they call tea here for a wake up in the morning."

Jack dug into his pouch. "You just became a very dear friend, DeAngelo. How much will I owe you for keeping me supplied with the elixir of life?" He caught the beer tossed his way and both humans plopped themselves in front of a circular raised fire pit for a chat.

Aneurin followed them inside. He spied Watash immediately. The huge silver and dark blue dragon was awake and reading a large tome in his nest stall. Aneurin put the basket by the door and quietly wandered over to Watash.

The old dragon winked and put down his book. "Good day to you, Aneurin! I've not seen you since you were fledged. How have you been? Flying well?"

"Not as much flying as I'd like, Watash." Aneurin kept to his human form and sat in a comfortable chair wedged in the stall area. There wasn't enough room for two dragons, unless Aneurin used the empty stall next to Watash. Besides, it was easier to have a private conversation this way. "So, what's the latest gossip from the mountains?"

The silver tip of Watash's tail lashed the ground for a moment, betraying his agitation. "Not good, I'm afraid. Being bonded has its disadvantages, and this is one of those times. We're not well trusted by the independent dragons. Even so, word filters down eventually." The dragon raised his head and stole a glance at the two laughing humans. "Don't tell our dear friends. This is none of their business yet. The Dragon's Stone is missing."

Aneurin bit his lower lip. He hated to admit his ignorance, so he pretended to be concerned. He'd ask Draig later what was the significance of the Stone. "That is bad news indeed. What's being done?"

Watash lowered his head and closed his eyes for a moment. "Nothing at present. A delegation of humans from the royal capital visited our queen at the time. Diplomatic relations are deteriorating rapidly between the non-humans and humans. The whole situation is like tinder in a dry forest. One small spark could set the whole thing ablaze, harming even the innocent. None of us wants that, no matter how much we hate King Cadell. We're putting a lot of hope into your…"

A crash of shattering glass cracked the air. "*King* Cadell?"

Aneurin started at the pure horror in Jack's voice. He jumped to his feet, guilt squirming in his stomach.

Jack stood at the entrance to the stall, his face white. In his hands were two beer bottles, one unopened and clearly for Aneurin. The remains of a third lay scattered at his feet, with beer soaking his white sneakers.

DeAngelo lit a cigarette, his eyes avoiding Jack's. "Yep. The bas… well, I don't think much of him, I'll say that, even though I work for him every winter, teaching."

Aneurin glanced at Watash, who gave him a warning glare. He got the message. Say nothing. Aneurin took the beer from Jack's hand. Under no circumstances should Jack be allowed to blurt out that Cadell was his father. "Thanks for the beer, Jack. Sorry you dropped one. Would you like a beer, Watash? I'll fetch another if you like."

The blue dragon picked up his tome. "No thank you, Aneurin. If you'll forgive me, I'd like to return to my reading, and DeAngelo needs to measure you for a saddle, I believe."

Dismissed, Aneurin took hold of Jack's arm and pulled his stunned friend back out to where DeAngelo waited, dragging on his smoke. Aneurin muttered under his breath, "Get hold of yourself, Jack. We'll talk later, privately."

Jack swallowed, and the shocked look left his eyes. "Your friend is right, Aneurin. It's getting late. Let's get this order for a saddle done." He took a long pull from the bottle. "I've still many questions to ask *Aunt* Lucynda tonight."

Aneurin winced. How Jack managed to keep it all straight that he must pretend Lucynda the Red Sorceress was supposed to be his aunt, not his mother, awed Aneurin. Even upset and angry, Jack maintained the lie. Dragons were too honest for fabrications, especially when it came to the complicated tales humans wove with ease.

DeAngelo stood and picked up a long cord. "You won't have much time, lad. You'll want to pack. We're leaving in a few days for the school. If you like, you can follow Watash and I so you don't get lost in the Troll Mountains. No fun, that. Colder than a witch's tit in an iron bra up there. The school has hot springs to keep it warm for our dragons, but outside of that limited area, Aneurin would die unless you know the way." He gestured to Aneurin. "Change form, would you?"

Aneurin meekly returned to dragon form and allowed DeAngelo to clamber up on one of his forelegs. He could feel the anger simmering just below Jack's cheerful mask. Jack was in for a shock when he realized the whole situation in Honalee, and Aneurin fervently wished he could be anywhere else that night when Jack found out the truth at dinner.

Chapter Three

Jack waited until they were all seated at the table in the hall and the menservants had dished out the first course. He barely glanced at it. "Mother, we need to talk."

The smile faded from Lucynda's face at his growling tone. Her blue eyes studied him for a full minute, at least. Then she sighed and put down her spoon next to her soup. "I was afraid of this. Go ahead. Ask your questions."

Out of the corner of his eye, Jack saw Aneurin share a telling and uncomfortable look with Draig. Too fucking bad if he made the dragons nervous tonight.

Jack ground his teeth and put a rein on his temper. The soup smelled savory, and his hungry stomach gurgled, but he'd be damned if he'd deal with this on a full stomach. He'd surely pay for it with a case of acid reflux if he took one bite given his level of frustration. "Why didn't you tell me Cadell was the king? Is that the reason for the lies about my being your sister's son?"

Lucynda looked down. "Yes, that's a large part of it. Forgive me. I'll have to use simple terms because you don't speak Honalean well. Draig and Aneurin will have to translate some of this." She turned and gabbled something to Draig he couldn't follow.

Draig cleared her throat. She dabbed her lips with the cloth napkin. "Keep in mind this is complicated and involves politics beyond your understanding, Jack."

Jack kept the irony out of his voice with difficulty. He could taste bile on the back of his tongue and wished for an antacid. "Yeah, I gathered that."

Aneurin ladled soup into his mouth with studied care and didn't meet his eyes. How much of this did the dragon already know? Why hadn't he said anything?

Jack's dear, conniving mother wrung and twisted her napkin in her hands until a rip developed along the edge. "My relationship with Cadell was only business. He'd provide me with a child in exchange for certain magic items I had in my possession at the time. He was just another wizard then. Once you were conceived, our business deal terminated. I sent his payment." She shrugged. "I had what I wanted. He had what he wanted."

Draig waded in. "Shortly after your conception, the queen requested the same service from Cadell. He was handsome, of a noble line, and respectful of her crown. Or so we thought. Lady help us, we all thought well of him then. To our shame, we even suggested him when the queen asked what male Lucynda had used."

A servant came in with the second course. Silence reigned while he served what smelled like a fish casserole.

Jack's stomach lurched uncomfortably. The stench of fish was never his favorite scent, but that odor was particularly foul. "What is this dish, if you please?"

Lucynda sniffed with apparent relish. "Ah, eel. My favorite." She permitted the servant to give her a large portion.

Draig grinned at Aneurin. "We keep them in the pond. Makes for a fun hunt when we want something fresh."

Visions of swimming with snake-like fish things didn't thrill him. Jack shuddered. He leaned over to Aneurin and muttered under his breath, "Remind me never to go swimming in the pond, will you?" Jack waved away the servant when he offered him some of the eel casserole.

Lucynda waited until the room was clear of servants before continuing. "Cadell played his game well. He used the months spent negotiating his contract with the queen very well. By the time the ink was dry, the entire court was enthralled with him and gave him all he asked in the contract." She took a bite of her casserole and chewed thoughtfully.

Draig cleared her mouth and picked up where Lucynda left off. "Most telling was the clause where he was permitted to stay at court to help raise his offspring." She coughed uncomfortably. "Male wizards are so rare, they are not socially obligated to remain and rear the offspring. They are expected to service as many sorceresses as ask for them, if possible."

Jack grimaced, recognizing the implied warning. He felt like he'd been dipped in ice-cold water. While Jack wasn't one of his more fanatical gay brethren who insulted females and considered them repugnant, he didn't consider himself a good candidate for putting out to stud, either. He fumbled for a diplomatic answer. "Not my idea of a good time, thanks."

Lucynda shrugged and gave him an understanding smile. "We're simply warning you. You're even more handsome than Cadell was in his youth, well built, and likely to be powerful once trained. Every sorceress within a hundred leagues will offer you the moon and stars for the opportunity of a night in your arms." She opened her eyes wide until she resembled a calf, and mimed romantic infatuation with razor accuracy.

Aneurin snickered.

His lips twitched, and Jack swallowed a chuckle until he choked. The humor of the situation finally struck him. "They're doomed to disappointment. The latest stud on the farm likes other studs." He reached out and grasped Aneurin's free hand. "Particularly one."

Draig snorted and shook her fork at him. "You say that now, but the first time Aneurin gets a whiff of a dragoness in musk… well, we'll see how strong your resolve is then, won't we? You'll be involved, like it or not, and you'd better have a willing body handy to --" She flushed.

Aneurin's fork clattered to his plate. His mouth fell open in shock. "I will? And Jack will feel it, too?"

Lucynda laughed at his white face. "You're bonded, aren't you? Dragons can't help themselves when it's time to mate. Even if Aneurin succeeds in fighting the urge to sky-fight for the right to mate, he'll still broadcast all the sexual urges, and he'll be locked in dragon form until it's over. Unless you have a willing partner, you'd better lock yourself in your rooms with all breakables elsewhere."

Jack grimaced, imagining himself groaning and spanking the monkey while every loose object whirled around the room in a mad dance. "Enough. I get the picture."

Draig winked at his discomfort. "Well, back to the subject of Cadell's treachery. You need to know why we're hiding you." She patted Lucynda's hand. "Let me explain in his language. It would be faster."

His mother nodded. "Perhaps so, but I think it would be best to cast a language spell on him before the night is out." She smiled at him. "We'll do it after dinner so you have time to recover before leaving."

Jack sighed and shoved the now cold soup aside. Oh, fun. He'd read enough books to assume he'd have a screaming headache. However, he recognized the need to have the full Honalean language impressed in his brain. School would be hard enough without a communication barrier. "Thank you, Mother."

Aneurin squeezed his hand and let go in silent support. Through their shared bond, Jack shared his disquiet with the revelations of the evening. Somehow, Jack knew the worst was yet to come.

Draig took a sip of the excellent wine served with dinner. "I'll make this quick and to the point. By the time the royal princess Miranda was born, Cadell had set himself up as the perfect royal consort and father. The court adored him, and the queen hung on his every word. The queen didn't have an easy pregnancy, and a worse birthing. She weakened and continued to bleed for days, dying less than a fortnight after Miranda's birth."

Jack frowned and didn't remind her of his world's royal families, who were so inbred that hemophilia was a common genetic flaw for generations. If Cadell was noble, there were probably quite a few gene crosses, more than enough to cause problems. Magic couldn't cure a genetic disease like that one. Even he could figure that out. He could almost see the next part coming, and Draig didn't disappoint him.

"That's when we learned of another term in the contract between the queen and Cadell. If the queen died before the child was old enough to take the throne, then he would be Regent for the child." Her lip curled. "He took the throne with unseemly haste, even before the queen was buried. Then Princess Miranda and her wet nurse went to the north tower. He trotted her out on state occasions for a few years, and then one day announced she was sick and asked the whole nation to pray. For weeks, healers and holy women filed in and out of the palace, to no avail. Princess Miranda was buried beside her mother in her sixth year. The wet nurse was never heard from again."

Jack huffed out a small, exasperated breath. Typical politics, just like Washington. It was five times as hard to unseat an incumbent who'd been in power just long enough for people to get used to him. As long as the politician caused no overt harm, his constituents would sit on their hands. "Cadell was by then the only ruler in town, and so firmly entrenched you couldn't remove him with dynamite, right?"

Lucynda, who'd frowned and listened intently, nodded. "I don't know what dyna -- what was it? -- is, but he's the closest legal thing we have to a ruler. Other than the fact that he's male, of course."

Aneurin and Draig both winced.

Jack's brow creased. "Okay, there's more to that statement than what's on the surface, isn't there?" He waited while the servants brought in the next course, mulling things over. This time, it looked and smelled like beef. He could live with that. Then it dawned on him. All the servants were male. All the shopkeepers he'd visited were female. Queen. He turned to Draig and spoke in English. "This is a matriarchal society and males are second class citizens?"

Draig shifted in her chair, and her chin jerked downward once.

Jack shuddered and cut up his dinner while he pondered the ramifications. He was the son of a hated usurper to the throne. However, no one knew that. No one but the people in this room, that sure. Jack thoughtfully shoved in a forkful of meat. Whatever it was, it was tasty. Sort of like beef. He switched back to Honalean. "Okay, I'm not happy with being a second class citizen, but I'll live." He wasn't obligated to stay in Honalee. He could go back to Washington any time. No need to hurt Lucynda. At least he wasn't in line for the throne or some stupid patriarchal lineage shit.

Lucynda smiled in relief, and the dragons relaxed. His mother waggled her fork in his direction. "In truth, you are a wizard, and so in a unique position. You are outside the normal --" She looked at Draig and added a few words Jack didn't know.

Draig hurriedly swallowed and finished for her in English. "She means social strata. Wizards and sorceresses have their own hierarchy. This is one of the reasons why we are so insistent on the school, Jack. Your ability to control magic is determined by levels of tests to demonstrate your power. Without the royal seals, you're considered just above a peasant hedge wizard, and that status is only gifted to you by virtue of your birth and what little was witnessed by Lady Tilda. Such poor control is just what keeps most men in low status. You'll have to prove you're better than that, or you will be treated as most men are in Honalee." Her glance flicked to one of the servants, who arranged more serving dishes on the sideboard.

Aneurin's mind voice filtered in, though he kept shoveling in food with single-minded intensity. "Males are assumed to be lacking in self-control, Jack. Some even consider us less intelligent, with notable examples. Reverse everything you're used to. Males are the home keepers, child tenders, and service staff. Females hold all positions of power, and it's enforced by the laws."

Jack put down his fork slowly as the full weight of this revelation settled in his stomach like cold lead.

He was used to being the object of prejudice because he was gay. That he could deal with, even if he didn't like it. Sexual orientation was not obvious unless you made it deliberately so. He'd seen even the worst raging queen "straighten up" when necessary. There was no disguising gender. Jack swallowed. Hard. Images of being black prior to the race riots of the 1960's fast-forwarded through his head. His left hand, thankfully out of sight in his lap, curled into a fist.

Aneurin jerked back, probably from the backlash of his rage. Plates and loose objects on the table rattled, as his anger translated into a magical manifestation.

He took a deep breath. "Excuse me. I need to take a walk." Jack forced himself to keep his voice calm, even though he could hear the icy sarcasm he couldn't disguise. He stood and threw his napkin on the table. One thing was clear. He had a mission beyond learning magic to protect his mother from a king bent on revenge, even above keeping him from breaking small objects whenever his emotions were out of hand. He had to prove his own worth. Now he wasn't just some abandoned orphan, determined to show the world he had a right to a place in it. Now he was part of an elite group of men who had the chance to prove equality of the sexes, or some shit like that. His head hurt.

Lucynda managed a regal nod, though she kept a wary eye on the rattling candlesticks. Aneurin and Draig both gave him sympathetic looks.

Jack stalked out of the room and slammed out the front door into the cool night air. His thoughts were so chaotic Jack didn't care where he went. He marched in a straight line toward a copse of trees just beyond the tilled areas of the gardens. No one was outside, and Jack made his way into the concealment without anyone noticing.

Without a clue how he would do it, somehow Jack had to prove men were equal. He stared up at the stars. He'd never given equality of the sexes much thought. Equality was a part of his life. "Where are you, Susan B. Anthony? Billie Jean King? Any advice?"

He found a large tree, leaned up against it, and slid down until his backside hit the grass. "Let's see. Mission one: get my magic under control. Check. Mission two: protect Lucynda from Cadell. How I'm going to do that, I haven't a clue. Okay, one day at a time on that one. Mission three: prove men are equal to an entire medieval matriarchal society." He threw his head back against the tree and saw more stars than there were in the night sky. "Boy, am I out of my depth."

* * *

Jack clamped his mouth shut to keep his teeth from chattering and hung on with grim determination to the odd iron loop that served in place of a saddle horn. He was more than grateful for DeAngelo's advice to wear gloves and his wraparound sunglasses. At least the saddle was the epitome of comfort and design, even if it was essentially a stuffed square cushion strapped to Aneurin's body. A secure buckled harness kept him firmly in his seat. Festooned with large decorative iron rings on the sides and behind, the saddle pad also served to hold the sturdy leather bags containing his clothes and wizard stuff.

In front and slightly to his left, DeAngelo waved and pointed down at a mountain lake any artist would give his left nut to paint. His black saddle, tooled with the familiar wings of Harley Davidson, had a set of motorcycle handlebars Jack eyed with envy. He even had black leather saddlebags hanging off the damn thing. Crazy old coot was a laugh and a half to hang with, and loyal to a fault.

Jack patted with satisfaction the brown leather bag containing his new camp percolator and six large bags of Seattle's best coffee, as well as the special travel mug DeAngelo had presented him with when they'd stopped by to pick up the saddle. Jack could survive anything as long as he had a coffee supply, even going to fucking school.

"Hang on. We're going to land." Aneurin's mind voice was excited.

Aneurin and Watash made a sharp turn to the left. Jack could now see what DeAngelo pointed at. It wasn't the lake, but a collection of stone buildings. Some were large and three stories high, others were squat single buildings, and one familiar dragon hangar. Extensive gardens, manicured and perfect, surrounded one building that also boasted a huge courtyard. Down by the lakeside, a gathering of people and dragons looked like some sort of medieval fair was in progress. He saw jugglers and an airborne stream of flame like a fire breather from a circus. The dragons lounged outside the mayhem in the sun or swam in the steaming lake. From the look of the way it bubbled, the lake was formed from hot springs.

"Quite a party going on down there." Jack still wasn't used to the telepathy thing, but even if the wind whipped away his voice, Aneurin heard him just fine.

"That's not a party. Watash tells me that's where the prospective students gather before something called the Trial of Wizard's Choice. DeAngelo says to land there and wait. Soon you'll be called to the main building and tested to see if you do have mage ability."

Aneurin backwinged, landing with only a small jolt outside the main circle of tents.

Jack dismounted. Trampled flat by the passage of both dragon and human feet, the meadow they'd landed in was bare of grass, and the steamy breeze from the lake was warm enough for him to shed his coat. Now that he was on the ground, the actions of the other students became clear. Some breathed fire like circus acts, some juggled objects by waving a wand, and others made things appear in mists. The crowd had the appearance of teenagers showing off. Meeting other student wizards wasn't appealing, and Jack seriously considered joining one fellow he saw lounging under the trees with a book in front of his nose. The solitary one had the right idea.

Instead, Jack turned his attention back to what Aneurin had said. "I'll be called? What about you?"

His pal laughed and changed form, shedding all his burdens in a heap where his back had been. He disentangled himself from the straps. "I'll probably hang around with Watash for a bit. I'm in school, too, so to speak. He's promised to tell me what to expect from the riding lessons." He gestured toward the pile of their belongings. "He did tell me servants would be along to get all this later, once you've passed the Trial."

Jack grimaced and studied this weird half-medieval world. The trees, grass, and mountains could have been anywhere in Europe, maybe the Alps or something, except for the steam rising from the lake. The word trial to him meant courts, lawyers, and criminal charges. He was spooked enough with the gender segregation thing. "Couldn't they call it a test? What kind of test?"

Aneurin shrugged and grinned. "Stop worrying. You win either way, don't you? If you don't pass their test, then Lucynda teaches you to control your magic. If you succeed, you'll learn here." He bent and kissed Jack gently.

"Trying to distract me with kisses, lover dragon?" Jack's lips tingled and twitched into a smile. He hated feeling this insecure, and itched for a bit of action. "I wish they'd get this over with."

Over Aneurin's shoulder, Jack saw a man approach the guy reading in the shade of a large oak. Whoever the intruder was, he didn't seem friendly. When the reader looked up, the newcomer snatched the book from his hands. Jack knew what a school bully was, and the reader seemed much smaller than his attacker.

Maybe he overreacted, but Jack hated bullies. The little short guy didn't stand a chance, and Jack wasn't going to just stand by and watch. He raced over just in time to hear the bully snarl, "You don't belong here, Remo. Why don't you go home?" The bully snatched at the little guy's cap.

Jack gave the short skinny Remo marks for pluck. He evaded the bully's hand and slapped at it. "It's none of your business why I'm here, Quenton. Leave me alone."

They both turned as Jack moved to stand by Remo, Aneurin right behind him. Geez, the shrimp even wore thick, gold-rimmed glasses. Whoever picked on short, skinny nerds in glasses deserved a punch in the mouth, so Jack glared at the muscular brunet named Quenton. "Yeah, why don't you go back to bragging with the other wannabes? Go breathe fire or something to show off instead of picking on guys shorter and weaker than you."

Quenton's lip curled. "You defend his wish to be here? Who are you to claim that right?" He tossed his greasy dark curls like some queen from Georgetown.

Remo gaped at Aneurin for a moment as if he could tell what Aneurin was. However, he was not afraid of standing on Jack's other side with his chin lifted. Nerd or not, the guy had balls. He pushed his glasses further upon his nose and spoke regally. "That's an impertinent question. You're no better than any other here, Quenton."

Jack curled his hands into fists, ready to knock this Quenton flat if it came down to brass tacks. Arrogant bastards like him Jack understood, especially when they were dressed in leather and silk. He caught on to the fact that Quenton might be noble, or at least rich. "Just call me Jack, and I don't give a damn about rank, privileges or other manure like that."

Quenton's eyes widened, and then narrowed speculatively. "We shall see." He reached over and snatched off Remo's cap.

White hair spilled out from the cap, obscuring Remo's face but not his ears. His pointed ears. He brushed his waist length hair out of his eyes and stood glaring defiantly at both Quenton and Jack. "Is there a law against an Elf wishing to learn human magic, now?"

Jack grinned, happy to finally meet an Elf. In fact, the cryptozoologist in him burned to talk to an Elf, but there were more important things at the moment. Jack shrugged cheerfully. "I wouldn't know, and I don't care. As far as I'm concerned, you can study any damn thing that interests you. Knowledge is never wasted."

Quenton threw the cap to Remo. "You've a great deal to learn, Jack. We'll see if you pass the Trial before continuing this conversation." He turned and stalked off.

Remo maintained dignity and bent to stuff his hair inside his cap before shoving it on his head. "So do you," he whispered to the retreating stiff back.

Jack put his hands on his hips and watched Quenton angrily shove between two tents and lose himself in the crowd. "Nice guy. Hope he doesn't end up as a classmate."

Aneurin tugged on Jack's sleeve to get his attention. "Now that's over, I'll take my leave and wait for word of your success. See you tonight." He kissed Jack once more before starting the long walk to the dragon hangar.

Remo's eyes followed him for a few moments. "Your dragon, Sir Jack?"

"Just Jack, thanks. Yeah. We've been together since I was born, more or less. His name is Aneurin." Jack walked over and picked up Remo's book, unsurprised to find it was written in an alphabet he couldn't hope to read. "Is this Elven?"

The Elf accepted the book and closed it. "Yes, of course." Then he smiled shyly. "Honalean isn't your primary language either, is it? You use words I do not know."

Jack gave Remo his best goofy grin. "You caught me. Hey, I'd rather hear about your people, if you don't mind. I've got coffee if we can get a fire going. You can tell me anything you want me to know."

Remo's grin grew wider and friendlier. "I do not know what this coffee is, and I would tell you many things, but I think the time of the Trial is at hand." He pointed to a gray-haired fellow resplendent in deep blue robes. It took Jack a few moments to recognize DeAngelo, walking purposely toward them.

They waited until DeAngelo came up to them, his robes swishing in the grass under the tree. Jack grinned to see the old biker looking like a storybook wizard.

DeAngelo winked at Jack and bowed formally to both of them. "As per the protocols, all noblemen and non-humans are requested to take the Trial first. Will you both follow me? Servants will attend to your luggage."

Remo's snowy eyebrow shot up, and he bowed gracefully. "Indeed? Well, then. Please lead us, good wizard."

Jack caught on, and did his best to bow, though he was sure he didn't do it as well. He stepped in to walk companionably by Remo's side, determined not to lose a chance for a chat with an Elf. From the surprised glance Remo shot him, he assumed he'd violated some protocol again. Screw their protocols.

DeAngelo snickered at Remo's shocked look. "I've no objections to you two coming in together, but you'll each face your Trial alone. Is that clear?"

Remo blinked and shot Jack an unfathomable look. "Of course."

Jack shrugged. He couldn't understand why Remo was acting like he'd been accorded some honor, but Jack really didn't care if he was breaking some sort of pecking order rule. "Clear as a bell, DeAngelo. Lead on."

The Elf smiled gently as they were led up the path through manicured gardens, but kept his thoughts to himself until they reached the gray granite steps of the largest building. Remo tugged on Jack's sleeve. "You'll want your wand, Jack."

Startled, Jack pulled his wand from the arm sheath DeAngelo had strapped to Jack's left forearm. "Why?"

DeAngelo chuckled and opened the door. "You may not need it, but we'll want to check it for mage properties. Here, give them to me."

Remo pulled his wand from the sleeves of his robe. For the first time, Jack noticed Remo wore a loose overcoat of a robe in blue silk, covered with silver embroidery. The front was open, and beneath he wore matching blue and white pants and shirt. Even his boots were blue. He handed his white wood wand over with a short, polite bow.

Jack gave the old biker wizard his simple brown wand, feeling strangely shabby in his jeans and tee shirt with the words "Lost in Thought. Please send a search party" emblazoned on the front in English. It was his private joke for DeAngelo and Aneurin. The old wizard had laughed like a loon this morning, but hadn't made Jack change into robes.

DeAngelo led them through the front entrance and through a large set of double doors to the right. Four other nervously fidgeting men sat in chairs, all dressed in robes heavily decorated with gold and silver embroidery. One of them was Quenton, who studiously ignored the newcomers and contemplated his fingernails. His ploy might have worked if his hands hadn't been shaking.

Odd objects like folded cloth, a candelabrum, a rock, and things Jack couldn't name covered a long table. Three thrones sat on the dais behind the table. Lady Tilda graced one, her baby pink robes covering her enormous chest. DeAngelo took one, and an old man who looked so frail a strong wind might blow him away occupied the other throne.

Remo and Jack looked at each other and shrugged. They crossed the floor and took two chairs where they'd have a clear view of what happened.

Lady Tilda stood and stepped regally over to stand behind the tables. "Good morning, my lords. This is the Trial of Wizard's Choice to determine if you have the necessary skills to learn from us. We will call your names one by one. At that time, please come forth and choose an object." She consulted a paper before her. "Lord Cale Aurelian, you are first."

A blond guy who would have fit every fairy tale description of the perfect Prince Charming rose from his chair and stepped confidently forward. He paced up and down the table for a few minutes, and then reached out to grab a fancy jeweled sword. He presented it to Lady Tilda with all the grace of a born courtier.

Lady Tilda tsked, and said coldly, "You failed. My apologies to your family, Lord Cale, when you return to them." She pointed airily out the door, and watched Prince Charming leave with his head bowed. She laid the sword aside and consulted her scroll. "Lord Quenton Beakmire."

Quenton marched forward defiantly, but took his time studying the contents of the table. Briefly, Jack caught a glimpse of his eyes. They were glazed and not really focused on any one object. Finally, he moved with deliberate care and touched a pile of yellow folded cloth. He seemed to nod to himself, and then took it to Lady Tilda as if he carried a treasure.

Lady Tilda accepted the cloth and laid it aside. "Pass." She pointed to a set of doors behind the thrones. "Go through those doors. Servants will show you to your rooms. You may spend the next few hours unpacking." DeAngelo handed him his wand as he passed by the thrones. The doors closed softly behind him.

Jack folded his arms across his chest and frowned. Great. Dipshit made it. What had he done that Prince Charming hadn't? Jack watched as two more noble lords tried their luck. Both chose objects after a quick study of the tables, but only Quenton hadn't looked at the objects themselves, but unfocused his eyes. Maybe he'd looked for something unseen? The two nobles each failed. What the hell had Quenton done? The spirit of competition was on Jack, and he couldn't let the slimy bastard win. Then it hit him. Something he'd read. What the hell -- he'd give it a shot when his turn came.

The two nobles took Lady Tilda's snotty attitude with more humility than Jack would have. She contemptuously dismissed them both with a sniff and pointed to the same doors Prince Charming had gone through. Once again, she consulted her paper. "Lord Jack Harringdon."

Jack jerked as he realized she meant him. He rose stiffly to his feet and ignored the sweat popping out on his forehead. One chance to be in a royal school where he might get one step closer to the man who had fathered him. One chance to make a success of himself in the land of his birth, or end up a stud stallion on the run from who knew how many women who wanted a one-night stand. And dammit, one chance to prove he was better than Dipshit Quenton. Jack glanced up and saw DeAngelo give him one wink. It helped to know he had a friend watching.

Remo leaned over and spoke quietly. "Good luck to you, Jack."

Okay, two friends. Time to see if his plan worked. Jack walked up to the tables, and pretended to take his time studying them. What he did was count how many paces it took to walk from one end of the tables to the other. Twelve steps. He turned and stalked back to the first end. Then Jack shut his eyes and held his hand out over the table. If his theory was correct, he'd know when he needed to stop.

Five paces, and his hand tingled for just a moment. Maybe, but it could have been just his hand going to sleep from being held in the same position. Jack hesitated, and then moved on. He could always go back.

Seven paces, and his hand tingled again. Stronger this time, but still not enough to be certain. Jack stopped for a moment to assess the sensation. If he moved his hand away, the tingling stopped.

He heard murmuring in the background, but ignored the sound. He refused to be distracted.

Just to be sure, Jack paced two more steps. This time, his hand was zapped. He snatched his hand back to his chest and sucked in his breath. "Damn, that hurt." Resolutely, Jack stuck his hand back out, prepared this time for the jolt of electricity like he'd stuck his finger in a light socket. Whatever it was, he was grabbing that item. His hand grasped a cool, round surface.

A humming sounded between his ears, and he felt for a moment like the whole world vibrated. He had the sensation of being dropped down a well, then falling into cupped hands. Hands that cradled him like a baby chick. He didn't much care for that analogy, but that was how he felt -- like something powerful held him in its grip. Unlike when Aneurin talked in his head and he heard words, this time he "heard" emotions. First, a curiosity, and then, satisfaction. The humming and vibration stopped. Jack staggered for a moment as the world seemed to shudder, then move on like a DVD on pause for a second.

What the hell just happened? Jack peeked. He'd chosen the fucking rock.

Chapter Four

Warily, Jack studied the simple oval of river rock. It lay quiescent in his hand despite the shock it had delivered moments before. Magic objects were weird, anyway. He walked the few steps to where Lady Tilda waited with her blue eyes as round as the stone. Now what had he done?

DeAngelo sat back with a satisfied smile splitting his lips and a mischievous gleam in his eyes. He gave Jack a short approving nod.

Lady Tilda all but snatched the rock out of his hands.

A baby's cry rattled Jack's ears. No one else gave any indication they'd heard the sound. Did the rock protest being separated from him? Oh, yeah, right. Like a rock needed a friend.

The lady finished her little rehearsed speech congratulating Jack and repeating the command to go through the double doors where servants awaited. However, her bright smile was full of malice and her blue eyes narrowed with what Jack interpreted as speculation. Her hands greedily clutched the rock like it was a fancy Faberge egg.

Jack spun around to wink at Remo, hoping the Elf got the message that he hoped he'd see Remo later.

Those incredible eyes of his twinkled congratulations, and Remo gave him a nod.

DeAngelo casually held out Jack's wand and the newly certified wizard took it like a trophy as Jack made his triumphant march past him. The doors opened automatically when Jack approached, and closed behind him with a soft thud.

The bare stone corridor was devoid of servants and decoration, just lamps flickering with odd little globes of light inside of them. To his left, the corridor stretched off into shadow, but Jack thought he saw a big grand staircase. To his right was a big window seat with a soft cushion, perfect for reading and storm watching on a winter night. Glass windows seemed incongruous in the medieval atmosphere of Honalee, but Jack wasn't about to argue.

A soft voice whispered in Jack's ears. "Go up the stairs."

He jumped and turned a full one-eighty. His heart thumped wildly, and Jack wondered if he'd ever get over his case of nerves. A servant in gray stood subserviently at his elbow.

"My apologies. I didn't mean to startle you." The man's voice never rose above a whisper. "Permit me to show you to your room, please." The man glided silently to the stairs down the corridor.

"Uh, okay. Thanks." Belatedly, Jack caught up with him. "Do you have a name?"

The man bowed. "My name is Casper, my lord wizard."

Jack followed Casper up two flights and down a series of more bare corridors. Within two turns, Jack was lost. "I hope you'll be kind to a new guy and show me around."

Casper paused in front of one open door. "I care for your room, my lord. However, I have access to the entire castle and grounds. Please step inside."

With some trepidation, Jack stepped into his bedroom. He didn't know what to expect, but two giant four-poster beds with curtains wasn't it. The fireplace wasn't lit, but a pile of wood stacked inside indicated it could be. Three chairs placed comfortably around the fireplace each boasted one of the odd little lamps hanging from the ceiling above a carved oak end table. "Cozy. I like it."

"Thank you. Goodbye for now, my lord." Casper bowed as he backed out, and the door swung shut silently.

"Jack!" Aneurin leaned over the arm of a chair Jack had thought empty. He stood and gave his bonded a spine-cracking hug. "I knew you could do it. Watash brought me up here to wait. Your Trial didn't take long."

Relief washed over Jack, and he returned the hug with a grin. He was in. He, the guy from the mundane world, was a wizard in a school for magecraft. "Yeah, it was easier than I thought. Just pick out a magical object off a table."

Aneurin raised one black eyebrow, his golden eyes flashing in the lamplight. "What did you choose?"

Jack chuckled. "A fucking rock." He stowed his wand in its sheath and rubbed his right hand. "Zapped me a good one, too." He opened his mouth to tell his dearest friend about the stone, but something stopped him. He coughed. What was it he was supposed to say? Dammit, he was slipping a groove. It had been important, too.

His dragon rubbed his chin and smiled. "To feel the energy in a stone is a rare skill. I am proud I bonded with a wizard powerful enough to feel the magic in rocks." Aneurin bent and kissed Jack. "Very proud."

Stone? Something about a stone flittered in his head for a moment, and then was gone. Giddy with relief and triumph, Jack batted his eyelashes and flirted like a drag queen. "Really, handsome? Do I get a reward for being a good boy and passing my Trial?"

The draconic purr Jack loved rumbled from Aneurin's chest. A distant thunder rumbling in the distance, warning of a storm to come, mingled with the sound of his anticipation. "I'm sure I can think of a suitable gift." His hand slipped between them to slide around Jack's waist and pull him fully against Aneurin's body.

His beautiful Aneurin, with his long, elegant fingers and heated whiskey-gold eyes, could fire Jack's blood like no other. Caressing his tight, sculpted buttocks through his thin cotton pants was pure pleasure for every one of his fingertips. "You speak with a forked tongue, dragon. How about kissing me with it instead?"

The two tips of Aneurin's tongue flickered out to tease Jack. He swooped down and hovered just above Jack's lips. "I think I shall."

"Shut up and do it." The room darkened, and the stout glass of the window behind Aneurin rattled. Jack didn't care what they did, as long as they celebrated Jack's success with a hot, sweaty, sexual romp. "A little less talk and a lot more action, lover." Jack reached up and grasped Aneurin's long dark hair in his fist, forcing the dragon man's head down.

Their lips met, accompanied by a loud crash of thunder. The sound of rain pattering on the glass heralded a storm both inside their room and out on the grounds. Jack shuddered and pulled Aneurin closer until it would take a crowbar to separate them. Jack doubted anyone would have the gall to try.

Aneurin threw an annoyed glance at the storm for interrupting. Those powerful hands that could and had shredded Jack's clothes from his body on previous occasions now lifted Jack's tee shirt from his waistband and slid beneath to rub his lower back, the long claw-like nails lightly scratching his skin.

Jack's back arched, just as Aneurin intended, and they broke apart. Jack's gaze locked on Aneurin's, breaking only while his lover whisked the shirt over his head and flung it across the room to land on the bed closest to the door. Jack nodded approval. Not that he cared. He'd have laid Aneurin's ass on the cold stone floor if necessary.

Aneurin reached for Jack's jeans, nearly snapping the buckle in his haste to undo his belt. "I find myself growing anxious."

Jack squirmed away from his hands, smiling evilly. His jeans rode around his hips, barely held up by his purple boxers. So they had a certain cartoon dinosaur on them. Ever try to get dragons on silk underwear? It was as close as he could come. Speaking of coming, Jack had things to do. He yanked at the long string holding Aneurin's tunic closed, and the lacing parted to reveal his chest almost to his navel. "Yum, yum. Dragon flesh to nibble on." Jack attacked his breastbone to another drum roll of thunder, and shoved Aneurin's shirt down his arms to pin them to his side. He tossed the string between the beds, out of reach.

His dragon drew a long, slow breath. "You omnivores will eat anything, won't you?"

He was too busy unknotting the drawstring holding Aneurin's britches up and filling his mouth with dragon nipple to answer, so he just hummed to drive Aneurin crazy. Aneurin couldn't hum. Purr, yes, hum, no. Something to do with the attachment of his tongue to his throat. Jack had never figured it out.

With his pants dropped around his ankles, Aneurin was gloriously naked except for the shirt holding his arms back to better display a massive chest as muscular as a television wrestler's. With six-pack abs to kill for, his lover was a sex crime waiting for a spot marked X. Aneurin waited with love in his eyes and his engorged cock at full attention.

Jack's cock twitched, anticipating burying itself between those firm globes of ass. He told it silently to wait. They'd get to see how sturdy the bed was soon enough. "Acres and acres, and it's all mine," Jack murmured to himself.

"Yes, I am. Just as you're my bonded." Aneurin struggled for a moment, unable to disentangle himself from the cotton shirt. "Help me out of this thing, would you? I'm stuck."

Jack's groin tightened, knowing something so strong as a dragon was momentarily trapped. What would a little light bondage hurt? They had a four-poster bed with square columns made from a single tree each. Jack wondered if Aneurin would like being tied to those posts. Jack shook his head. "I kind of like seeing something as strong as you temporarily helpless. I want to fuck you like that."

Aneurin's eyes flew open wide and a fire lit behind them. Conflicted emotions played across his face. "You like having power over a dragon?"

Jack was startled by the fear in his eyes. Perhaps dragonkind had a thing against any sort of servitude. God knew, Aneurin had an independent streak a mile wide. Jack hurried to caress his chest reassuringly. "Easy, Aneurin. I know you could flex those chest muscles or change form, and be out of it in a heartbeat. It's just a game, that's all. I know in many ways I'm smaller and weaker than you, so pretending to turn the tables excites me. That's all."

Aneurin studied his face for a moment, and then relaxed. "Oh. Well, then. Since we're just pretending I'm helpless, I suppose that's all right."

Jack's hand slid over to tweak one of his nipples. Aneurin's eyelids half-lidded, and that huge purple cock Jack intended to swallow later bumped his thigh, they were standing so close together. "As long as you're willing, we'll play this way. The second you're uncomfortable, say something and I'll help you out of that tangle. I promise."

Aneurin's tongue flickered out of his mouth. He knew what that thing did to Jack in either form his dragon lover was in. "Are you going to stand there with your jeans hanging off your butt and your purple underwear showing, or are you going to do something?"

Jack looked down at his pants riding his hips and threatening a slow slide down. "You could remove them for me, you know, if they bother you so much." Jack shook his finger at Aneurin's long nose. "No magic."

Aneurin was still for a moment. "How? With no magic and my hands unavailable to caress you?"

Jack arched one eyebrow and kept his face serious, enjoying this little role-play. Yeah, Aneurin could kick his ass with one buffet of his wings or a sweep of his tail if he wanted, but his dragon chose to be weakened temporarily. The thought made all the blood rush to Jack's groin, and his head swam for a moment. "Use your imagination, or better yet, use your tongue."

Those golden eyes glittered as he figured it out. Aneurin smiled wickedly and knelt, his face and that mobile tongue inches from Jack's full yearning cock. Aneurin leaned over to pull one side of Jack's jeans by the belt loop until the whole thing fell around his ankles.

A cool breeze assaulted Jack's silk boxers, and a peal of thunder announced a spatter of hard rain on the window. Castles were notoriously drafty structures, and Jack paid with a chill wind on his silk-covered ass. He shivered, partially from the cold and partially from anticipation. Jack playfully tugged on Aneurin's hair. "Evil dragon. Stop teasing. I'm freezing."

"And I'm not? I remind you I'm the naked reptilian." Swiftly Aneurin turned and spat a long gout of flame into the fireplace, igniting it with one breath. A taper candle on one of the tables slowly bent, melting in the heat. The chair next to it smoked, but didn't catch fire.

Jack yelped and leapt back. His heart thumped in his chest at having his jewels that close to something so incredibly hot. Jack liked danger, but the reminder that his most treasured possessions were about to be swallowed by something that had a furnace inside was both exhilarating and terrifying all at once.

Aneurin batted those long black lashes at Jack innocently, and gave him a toothy smile. "Just a reminder this is only a game."

Swallowing hard, Jack put his hand to his chest and took a deep breath. "Dragons are so unpredictable. Okay, I get the message." Jack stepped back into position, but braced one leg against the arm of the nearest chair. He knew how easily Aneurin could make his knees weak.

Moving with all the speed of his reptilian nature, Aneurin took Jack's aching cock into his mouth and sucked. Hard. His forked tongue slipped beneath to tickle and caress Jack's balls.

Jack moaned, threw his head back, and gave himself to Aneurin's not so tender mercies. "Let's move this little party to the bed, shall we?"

* * *

Cold air hit Jack's cock. Aneurin's warm mouth was gone, and the fire wasn't doing a damn thing to improve the stone-cold temperature of the room compared to the furnace inside his dragon. Love filled his heart for the one constant in his changed life. Aneurin was more than sex partner and transportation in this crazy circumstance. He was his friend, his sanity, and the other half of his soul. Jack reached down and helped him off the floor.

Aneurin's whiskey gold eyes looked at him with love and trust. He wobbled a bit, and his skin was icy cold. His draconic nature made him more susceptible to temperature, and apparently, the fire wasn't warming him, either. "Thank you."

Those two slurred words told Jack how close he was to torpor. Jack brushed Aneurin's long dark hair out of his face, feeling very guilty. Somehow, his knowledge of dragonkind had been increased. He knew much more than Aneurin had ever told him. "Come on, lover dragon. Let's get your body as warm as the furnace in your gut."

His dragon allowed Jack to lead him to the bed, and Aneurin tumbled bonelessly on the burgundy velvet bedspread. He gave Jack a sleepy smile. "You'll heat me up. You always do."

"Yeah, I will." With Aneurin's arms still tangled in his shirt behind him, he was Jack's fantasy come to life. Aneurin's wing muscles translated into a broad chest with firm pectorals the size of small dinner plates when he was in human form. The rest of him was long, lean, and languid like his lizard relations, though Jack doubted Aneurin would appreciate the comparison. His proud dragon lay displayed before him, a feast for the taking. Hunger to taste Aneurin overwhelmed him, and Jack bent to sample his dragon's mouth.

Aneurin willingly opened his lips and allowed Jack's tongue entry. Their tongues tangled, not like a battle to see who dominated, but more an exploration of taste and texture. Aneurin's eyes shut halfway, and he gave himself to Jack's will.

Nothing could have aroused Jack more. Fevered lust rocked him, and the human sucked in a breath to maintain control before taking his lover with primal need. Gently, gently, Jack told himself. He wanted to show Aneurin his love and gratitude for the dragon's trust and friendship. Jack owed him more than he could say for leaving Aneurin behind all those years, and wondered if he'd ever make it up to the dragon. Jack moved to lick and kiss those still-hollow cheeks from years of starving without him and vowed to take better care of his dragon. "Such a skinny dragon, you are," he teased. "You need to eat more."

Aneurin rewarded his joke with a chuckle. "I'll hunt with Watash and the other dragons while you're in class tomorrow. They tell me there's fine fat deer within the safe zone and fish in the lake to dive for."

Visions of graceful dragons diving from the air like cormorants flickered in front of Jack's eyes. Where had that vision come from? He could see it clear as day, like a scene from a movie. He sat on the edge of the bed and moved Aneurin's silky black hair aside with his left hand so he could nibble on Aneurin's ears and neck. "Dry off in the sun before we have flying lessons, will you? I don't fancy a wet ass."

Aneurin moaned and turned his head to allow Jack better access. "Saddle. You'll have a saddle." He writhed in his bonds. "Dammit, Jack, get up here and fuck me."

Jack chuckled and reached into his bags beside the bed. The dark brown one held his lube, condoms, and a special present he'd saved for just such an occasion as this. "Not yet, Aneurin, but I will. First, a little gift from me." His hand closed around the distinctive bullet-shaped bottle. He brandished it in front of his dragon's curious face.

Frowning, Aneurin read the label without comprehension. "What's a warming liquid?"

"A special substance with properties you're going to like, I hope." Grinning, Jack flipped the cap. The scent of blackberries filled the air, and he allowed one drop to fall on his fingertip. Lazily, he rubbed it on Aneurin's right nipple, nearest to him.

The nipple hardened immediately beneath his fingertip. Aneurin squirmed. "By my foremothers, that feels good."

Wickedly, Jack leaned forward until his lips hovered inches above the gooey delight. Oh, this was going to be a pleasant surprise. "Just wait and see what happens next." He blew a hot breath of air across the nipple.

Aneurin's back arched as he tried to lift himself off the bed with an inarticulate cry of pleasure. "Hot! It got hot!"

His hand still resting on the dragon's chest, Jack pushed him back down on the mattress. Aneurin's reaction was even better than Jack had dared hope for. "So you like my version of dragon breath? There's more."

Gasping for air, Aneurin was helpless to stop Jack. "More? Shards, I can't take much more."

"Yes, you can." Jack bent to lick a tasty mouthful of blackberry-flavored nipple before sucking it in. Where Aneurin couldn't see, Jack dribbled more of the tasty liquid into his right hand, and slid it toward Aneurin's rigid cock.

Moans escaped Aneurin's throat, and changed to draconic purrs when Jack's slippery hand encased his cock and stroked the fluid up and down the entire length. Quickly, Aneurin matched his movements to Jack's, timing his thrusts into Jack's hand to increase the pleasurable sensation of the slick liquid. "Ja -- ah -- ack!"

Aneurin's shirt snarled as it ripped in two, unable to contain a dragon in the throes of passion. Oh, well, bondage on a dragon was always going to be a fragile thing. Jack still had Aneurin at his mercy, sort of.

Jack released Aneurin's nipple and licked his way down the dragon man's flat, hairless belly. He reached his goal of Aneurin's thick, appropriately purplish cock. After all, his dragon body was purple. Aneurin's fingers tightened in Jack's hair, begging for his mouth.

Jack winced and withdrew teasingly. His mouth watered to taste a blackberry flavored dragon dick, but Jack would be damned if he'd end the game by giving his dragon any control. The word *control* echoed back to him in his mind. This wizard shit was getting to him.

"Dammit, Jack, stop tormenting me." However, Aneurin released his grip on Jack's hair.

Jack chuckled. His eager lips wrapped around the head of Aneurin's cock and his taste buds exploded with blackberry-sweet meat. Now Jack lay fully upon the bed between Aneurin's legs, and ground his dick into the velvety bedspread.

Aneurin yelped and thrust upward, shoving his cock deep down Jack's throat in a convulsive movement. Had Jack not been prepared, he might have gagged.

Jack's right hand, still sticky with the warming solution, crept down to play with Aneurin's tightening balls. Already the dragon's body prepared to pop off a load, and Jack wanted Aneurin to come first. Jack's other toys could wait for another day, another opportunity. Deliberately, his middle finger played with Aneurin's ass. He thought hard at his dragon, "I love you, Fireball Butt."

Bless those thick stone walls for absorbing the sound of a dragon's ecstatic shriek. Jack's ears rang, his throat filled, and he swallowed in a big hurry to keep from choking. Hungrily, Jack took it all in. His own need pulsed in time to his attempts to drill a hole in the mattress beneath him.

His dragon lover convulsed like an epileptic in full seizure before collapsing limply into the center of the bed. Aneurin's one long roar subsided into harsh, growling pants. When he could stand no more, Aneurin grabbed Jack's ears and tugged until Jack lifted his head.

Jack licked his lips and gulped down the last tasty drops. "How does a dragon hold his liquor?" Jack paused. "By the ears."

Aneurin stared for a full three heartbeats before his eyes flew open wide as he caught the joke. He could barely laugh around his gasps, but at least he let go of Jack's ears before his claw-like nails gave his human new places for earrings Jack didn't want. "Shut up and fuck me, you damned wizard."

The "damned wizard" snickered and knelt on the bed to grab Aneurin's ankles, enjoying how the dragon's toes curled in anticipation. With one hand, Jack slathered his cock with some of the solution, foregoing the condom since Aneurin wasn't susceptible to disease like a human partner. Besides, Jack was too anxious to wait.

Still in the throes of passion, Aneurin lifted his legs and did his reptilian best to bend himself in half. He was a damn sight better at it than a human would be, since his spine was twice as flexible. "Hard, Jack. Give it to me hard."

Too pent up to wait any longer, Jack slammed into Aneurin's ass with as much force as he dared. Getting past the first barrier was easy enough, but he refused to cause his dragon internal damage by shoving all the way in without giving Aneurin time to adjust. Jack didn't give a rat's ass that Aneurin's insides were built to withstand an internal furnace.

Heated dragon tissue closed around Jack's cock. Warm oven mitts, straight from delivering a pizza to the counter, had about the same barely tolerable temperature. Aneurin threw his arms around his legs to hold them steady, his whiskey eyes hazed with lust.

Now Jack wished he could roar with pleasure, but all that came out was a long groan. Heat and pressure enveloped his over-stimulated cock in pure sensation. The scent of their play combined with the aroma of blackberries, as much a taste as a smell. A reverent "Bloody hell!" fell from his mouth without passing through his brain. Jack tightened his buttocks and slid home as soon as the barrier allowed.

Aneurin sucked in a breath, his head thrown back and his mouth open in a silent roar. He grasped his hands over Jack's and pulled his ankles in tighter, wordlessly begging for more.

Unable to maintain any sort of control, Jack pounded into Aneurin like a jackhammer. There was no stopping his thrusts, and Jack didn't want to in any case. Every inch of him screamed with need for release with his nerve endings burning, maybe literally, inside the fiery insides of his love. Not lover. Love. No one else came close to fulfilling all Jack's needs, no one else had almost died for him. Jack poured all that love into every stroke, waiting for the final giving his heart demanded.

His wonderful dragon smiled ecstatically. Aneurin must have sensed this extra dollop of emotion on top of their physical play through their bond. Nothing else could explain why he suddenly roared and came again all over Jack's chest in great gouts of white cream.

Now Jack screamed. His poor human vocal cords were unable to match the draconic expression of pleasure and happiness, but they gave vent to the closest thing Jack could manage. Something he couldn't name reached out and seized him, but he could sense it meant no harm.

Aneurin's orgasm soared up their bond, a few seconds of disorientation, and an electric shock that sent Jack straight over the cliff edge and into flight. In that moment of shared pleasure, Jack could have sworn they were both dragons, mating on the wing high above the mountains where the air was so cold Jack could see his breath as they roared and fucked mindlessly in shared passion. In the sane back of Jack's mind, something celebrated and he knew his dragon body was real.

Neither of them cared they could not even soar, but rather plummeted toward the earth. The rush of adrenaline coursed through Jack's body, heightening every sensation. They careened to certain death, uncaring and unwilling to stop.

At the last possible moment, Aneurin's wings snapped open and his forearms wrapped around Jack to glide them gently to the lakeside opposite where the humans still partied wildly. Their bonfires winked and lit the lake water with beautiful colors of flame, and the sweet aroma of smoke scented the air.

They chuckled indulgently as if watching children's antics, and rested their entwined bodies atop a delightfully cushioned meadow of bushes that creaked and snapped like firecrackers as they settled.

Somehow, Jack knew their bodies could not part yet, and he was content to remain locked in Aneurin's embrace. Jack sighed, and purred, surprising himself. "Aneurin?"

A sleepy golden eye opened and looked down his purple snout at Jack. "Hmm?"

"What color am I?" Out of his subconscious popped that weird question instead of asking Aneurin if dragon love was like this all the time. Somehow, Jack knew the answer to both.

Aneurin's tongue flickered out to caress Jack's muzzle. "Black, Jack. Black as the night. Go to sleep. You have class tomorrow." His huge purple wing settled over his bonded like a blanket.

Jack snuggled and twined his long neck around Aneurin. His last conscious thought was stupid, but Jack couldn't help wondering, didn't black dragons breathe sulfuric acid? "That might explain my acid reflux."

Another voice laughed with Aneurin's chuckles at the joke. An image formed in Jack's mind. The stone. That damned stone he'd touched. What the hell was it? For a brief moment, an image of the rock, just as he'd held it in his hands at the Trial, appeared. Then the stone morphed into a tiny golden dragon. Seconds later the images were gone, and with it, the memory of the stone's special nature. *Later*, it promised. *Later*. Sleep stole over Jack before he could ask any more questions.

Chapter Five

Aneurin opened one sleepy eye when the first birdsong of the morning began from a lark on their windowsill. The first rays of a pink dawn speared up on the horizon, but hadn't completely chased away the darkness yet. He let the bird finish its song and flitter away, considering it a victory tune in celebration of not only Jack's acceptance into the Royal Academy, but also Jack's unprecedented transformation into a dragon. His bonded was truly remarkable, and completely unaware of how gifted he was.

Jack snuffled and rolled over on his back, losing a large portion of the blanket in the process. He lay with his cock pointing at the canopy above them, displayed in all his glory with his right hand under his head in an unconsciously erotic pose.

The dragon in man form eased away from his lover wizard and quietly rose from the bed. A washstand nearby probably contained water, since a small stack of folded towels sat next to it. The idea of washing Jack clean and continuing their play until breakfast brought a sly smile to Aneurin's lips.

The room was a mess of clothing tossed haphazardly aside, leather bags scattered on the floor, and the fireplace gone cold and ashy in the soft gray light of dawn. Even the other empty bed had lumpy piles stacked on it, though Aneurin couldn't remember putting anything there the night before. The dragon stepped gingerly over the detritus of their play and poured water from the pitcher as quietly as he could into a kettle from the hearth.

Rather than waste time starting a fire and chance waking Jack, Aneurin set the kettle on the hook in the firebox and blew gently on it with his fiery breath until steam rose from the neck.

Mixing cold and warm water together in the provided bowl took only a few moments, and shortly Aneurin squeezed out a soft linen square he found on the shelf of the washstand. He washed himself, enjoying the familiar scratch of linen on his sensitive cock. It was nice to be back among simple things he understood instead of the crazy world Jack had come from. Aneurin would never completely understand "civilization" where noise was a part of everyday life and humans reacted to the sounds of bells, alarms, and horns like well-trained animals.

Since coming to Honalee, Jack had alternated between discomfort and fascination, sometimes clenching his jaw with determination to learn the world of his birth. At other times he acted like a child on holiday, eager to learn and oblivious of danger.

Aneurin despaired of protecting Jack from all who would harm the son of the king when Jack romped about happily learning all he could of the different races inhabiting Honalee. Worse, Aneurin himself had not grown to maturity in Honalee either, and lived in fear he'd miss some detail that could spell Jack's death. Aneurin shook his head, sighed, and began washing his bonded.

Jack's eyes flew open at the first touch of the cloth, and he jerked as if he'd been shot with an arrow. His deep green eyes focused on Aneurin and softened with love. He chuckled softly. "Insatiable dragon."

Love slid up their bond and made Aneurin tremble with the depth of emotion. Food for his soul, more important than meat, filled him. Since regaining his sight and strength, Aneurin feasted as much on the excess energy pouring from his wizard's body as he did on the excellent food fed to him by his loving human. He grinned and winked at Jack. "You know what a carnivore I am. How can I resist such a tasty feast before me?" He knelt beside the bed to take in Jack's now rock hard phallus.

Jack groaned and relaxed, trustingly giving himself to his dragon.

A rustle came from the other bed. The lumps that Aneurin had thought were their luggage moved, and a grass green eye curtained by white hair appeared from under a blanket. "Yum, yum. Will you share?"

At the soft question from the other bed, Aneurin stopped sucking and peered over Jack's hip without releasing the tasty delicacy in his mouth. In his eagerness to celebrate Jack's victory, he'd forgotten Watash's warning that they would share their room with another of the adult male students.

Startled, Jack looked over his shoulder, flushing bright red. Jack cleared his throat, but didn't remove his cock from Aneurin's slackened mouth. "Uh, hi Remo. What did you say?" Jack fumbled with the bedclothes in an attempt to cover himself and Aneurin, but was thoroughly tangled.

Aneurin blushed and winced guiltily. He'd forgotten to even taste the air for unfamiliar scents in his eagerness to further cement his bond with Jack. The handsome Elf could easily have been an assassin instead of a fellow student.

Remo rose from the bed, and knelt next to Aneurin. His large, grass colored gaze focused on the dragon man, and Aneurin saw the plea in his eyes. "Please, will you share?" He colored as brightly as they. "I've never had a dragon and a human before. I hope I don't offend by my request."

Aneurin's jaw dropped in surprise, and Jack's softening cock fell out of his mouth. Conflicting emotions surged around his head and heart. One was an unreasoning jealousy. Another was the lust for the Elf he'd kept hidden since Aneurin first laid eyes on his graceful beauty. Third was self-disgust for feeling these things at all.

Several emotions flittered across Jack's face, and his heated cock twitched, brushing Aneurin's cheek. Through their bond -- at this distance, Aneurin easily sensed everything his bonded felt -- the same emotions coursing through him roiled in Jack. "Uh, not exactly what I meant when I said I'd see you again, Remo. Aneurin? What do you want?"

Bless Jack for being polite enough to emphasize his dragon's wishes were paramount. Aneurin could smell the arousal coming from them both, and squelched the jealousy firmly. There was no harm in allowing the Elf to play with them. In fact, it might be a good thing, since Remo was to share their room. He smiled at Remo. "Certainly you may join me for my unusual breakfast. Jack has tangled himself in the linens and is at our mercy."

Remo squirmed on his heels for a moment, lust darkening his eyes to the color of moss. He clapped his two fists together in front of Aneurin's face. "Oh, yes. Bind me, too, then. I love this game, and have played it many times."

Jack sat upright in the bed. For the first time, Aneurin could not read what was in Jack's mind. A barrier had been erected within his heart, as if he closed off something he did not want to feel. He reached down to the floor and picked up the lacing that had held Aneurin's tunic together. With the air of a ceremony, he wound it loosely around Remo's hands and put the ends where the Elf could grasp them. "It seems symbolic that I tie you with Aneurin's lacing, and give you the same right of freedom whenever you want it." He grasped the tops of Remo's hands. "Aneurin and I both bind you until you wish to be free. Fair deal?"

Remo nodded happily, with a dazzling smile.

The jealousy in Aneurin's heart melted away at Jack's proclamation. His bonded included him in permitting the Elf to join their play and made Remo his equal in the temporary and voluntary confinement. With the jealousy gone, lust returned full force to life within his body. "Enough wasting time." Aneurin removed Remo's tunic and soft pants with magic, and placed them neatly on the other bed.

Jack rose from the bed to his feet, and offered his cock to Aneurin with one hand and crooked his finger at Remo with the other. "Come here, sexy Elf."

Remo stood and shook the shining mass of silvery hair out of his eyes. His body was pale, but lightly tanned from the sun, except where a loincloth might fall to give his tenderest parts some protection. There, his skin gleamed like milk in moonlight.

For a brief moment, Aneurin wondered what that milky flesh would taste like. Would it be as sweet as it looked? He'd soon find out, but for now he was offered meat he knew well and wanted. He sucked down Jack's cock happily.

Twisting his upper body without disturbing what Aneurin did, Jack put his arms around Remo and drew him closer. "I have to ask. Is it true Elf ears are very sensitive?"

Remo swallowed hard, strangling inarticulately for a moment on his words, and then whispered, "Yes."

Aroused by the byplay above him, Aneurin felt his own cock heat and engorge. From his position on the floor, the dragon could see little, but he had better things to do while he listened. The sweet taste of man flesh filled his mouth, and he nursed the head of Jack's tasty cock with relish. Soon, they'd have the human on his back again where the Elf and dragon could roam before pleasing themselves. Aneurin had never played with anyone else, and the uncertainty of how to include another filled his mind with many exciting possibilities. Aneurin devoutly hoped it would be his cock in the Elf's ass while Jack filled his, but who knew what would happen? The dragon sucked harder, so filled with arousal he feared he'd burst.

Jack hoisted the lightweight Elf high in the air, until Remo's bare feet brushed Aneurin's shoulder. Knowing Jack's preferences for a mouthful of nipple, Aneurin assumed Jack tasted the white flesh and berry brown buds.

Remo moaned, and his toes curled, so Aneurin could safely think the Elf found as much pleasure in Jack's tongue and teeth as his dragon did.

The room crackled and snapped with mage energy as the two untrained wizards vented their excess energies. The power moved around and along his body, as if Aneurin had stepped in a nest of ants that investigated the new structure without stinging. Dragons could not be harmed by ordinary magic, and certainly neither of these two could command -- yet -- the greater magic that could affect him, so he could merely watch for flying objects without fear. He could probably contain the energies, if it came down to it.

Aneurin heard the slide of flesh on flesh, and Remo's body twitched. The lusty dragon looked up to see the Elf now riding a wave of energy, completely unaware he did so. Remo's head was thrown back until his long hair fell to brush his hips, while Jack's hand supported the milky ass and delved into the crack to tickle and tease.

Jack was aware he levitated the Elf, it seemed, for he kept one arm firmly wrapped around Remo's waist, holding his play "victim" steady while his mouth sank lower to tease the firm slender belly.

Aneurin chose to lick and nibble down to Jack's balls, and found them rising steadily upward as well, in preparation for an explosion of pleasure. This would not do, for the mage energy pulsing in the room warned Aneurin an explosion of another sort was a real possibility. Whether it came from Jack alone or the Elf did not matter. Aneurin didn't feel like watching them immolate themselves in their passion. Aneurin released Jack's cock from his attentions. "I suggest we continue this while lying upon the bed."

Remo was the first to hear his words. His head snapped upright, and he looked around. The Elf's blue bag whizzed by his head, doing a mad dance with an unlit candle. "Oh, dear. Perhaps we should."

Aneurin's bonded raised his head from Remo's flesh, his eyes glazed and unseeing. Jack grunted when a small table collided with his back. Awareness returned to his moody dark eyes. "Ouch. Damn. Forgot about that." In that instant, all objects stopped their movement and fell to the floor.

That included Remo, and Jack's grip on his ass and waist was insufficient to hold him. An undignified squeak of alarm heralded his plummet to the floor.

Aneurin cushioned Remo before real damage could ensure the end of their play, though they ended up in a tangled heap on the icy flagstones of the floor. Oh, yes, Aneurin could see the Elf was sweet to hold, with firm long muscles beneath that moonlit flesh. His arousal was such the images of impaling that sweet body on his cock sprang to Aneurin's mind before he could consider the unworthiness of the thought.

For his part, Remo took the indignity with grace. He used his bound hands to push himself off Aneurin's chest, and sat upon the dragon's cock until he rubbed his cock with the dragon's, creating sweet agony. Remo's bright eyes twinkled, and he bent to give Aneurin a short kiss. "Thanks for breaking my fall, dragon. You are most kind."

Jack lifted Remo off Aneurin with a worried frown. "Are you both okay? Nothing broken? Let's get off this floor before Aneurin goes into a reptilian torpor." He set Remo gently on the floor next to Aneurin, and then Jack put both hands out to aid his dragon in rising.

Remo rushed to assist, and Aneurin was soon off the achingly cold floor. Now the Elf took command, his maidenly shyness a thing of the past. He addressed Aneurin. "I think Jack should fuck you first, do you not, Aneurin? If you will see to his pleasure, I shall cast a shield spell around the bed so we'll be safe from flying furnishings. I've ability enough for that, I think."

Aneurin had no doubt an Elf could do more than that, but he nodded his agreement. Aneurin's eyes narrowed a trifle as he remembered Elves learned magic from the cradle, though non-Elven eyes rarely saw it. Why would an Elf wish to present himself to learn human wizardry, anyway? Aneurin would ask Remo privately later.

Jack kissed his dragon, then Remo. "I'll leave myself in capable hands, then." He eyed Remo's bonds. "Or should I say, other appendages?" He laughed and sat down on their bed, reaching onto the nightstand for the equipment he felt essential to play -- condoms and lubricant.

Remo met Aneurin's appraisal blandly, batting his eyes like a flirting wench. "The morning flies by, and today we plunge into a whirlwind of new knowledge. Let's enjoy while we can. There will be time enough for conversation as the days pass, I am sure." He leaned forward to whisper, "I am anxious to be beneath a dragon. Hurry."

Aneurin controlled his laughter with difficulty and told his treacherous body to resist for a moment longer. His cock developed a mind of its own and yearned toward Remo. His anus puckered at the sound of his rider's groans as Jack anointed himself with lubricant for their mutual pleasure. Aneurin reminded himself to borrow some for Remo's sweet ass. The devious Elf was up to something, and Aneurin vowed to keep that firmly in mind to discuss with Jack at the first opportunity. Such thoughts did not wither his desire for the graceful being before him, but the dragon would remain wary. For now, he would play the game. Aneurin turned to Jack. "May I borrow some of your lubricant?"

Unaware of his concerns, Jack raised one dark eyebrow and slathered Aneurin's heated cock generously with the warm, slick liquid. Jack's chameleon eyes weren't dark moody green now, but nearly as blazing gold as Aneurin's own with lust. His lazy grin was full of promise. "Going to be the fulcrum between us, Aneurin?"

"That is a plan I like!" Remo slipped to the other side of the generous bed and laid his head upon the velvet coverlet. His shining length of hair spilled over the pillows like silken embroidery. He crooked an enticing finger at Aneurin despite his bound wrists. "Come inside and play, dragon. Be the full crumb, whatever that is."

While Jack roared with laughter, Aneurin clambered awkwardly on the bed and between Remo's knees. Despite his earlier lust, things were moving just a bit quickly for his taste.

Remo helpfully put his ankles in the air, amazingly almost touching his nose. "I am stronger and more flexible than I look. Do not think you will harm me."

Jack stifled his chuckles and shoved gently at Aneurin's back. "Have at Remo, and once you're firmly planted, I'll enter you." He kissed Aneurin's shoulder. "I think you'll have to be the one to move between us for this to work."

The thought of stroking in and out of the Elf while impaling himself on Jack's thick cock was more than Aneurin's lust could bear. Aneurin took his aching penis in both hands and began his gradual journey into Remo's willing depths.

Jack left their bed for a moment and returned with Remo's glasses in his hands. He slid them on the Elf's astonished face with a sheepish grin. "Hope you don't mind, but I think they're sexy."

Blushing furiously, Remo blinked at Jack. Then, as if he could no longer contain himself, his eyelids fluttered half shut. "As you --" He stopped and moaned. "-- wish."

Aneurin slid completely within the Elf and echoed his incoherent moans of appreciation. Remo's body throttled his cock with sweet agony. Aneurin's balls ground against his firm ass cheeks, begging for release. The dragon silently agreed with Jack that their new friend was twice as enticing with the lenses magnifying his luminous eyes. Aneurin grasped Remo's cock to give the Elf release with his hand and waited for Jack's assault on his own receptive body.

Jack wasted no time, impaling Aneurin as quickly as he could without damage. The human's breath hissed behind Aneurin. "This feels fantastic. I'm not going to last worth a shit, guys."

They did not prolong their pleasures. For a few minutes the room echoed with their harsh gasps and collective cries of pleasure. Vaguely Aneurin noted there were no crashes of crockery hitting the walls. He assumed Remo's shielding of the bed had worked, though Aneurin had not seen him cast a spell.

Only a few short thrusts, and Aneurin felt his balls scream with release. He buried himself in Remo's body and roared his pleasure. The dragon's clawed hand mindlessly stroked Remo to match his own cries of pleasure.

Jack followed them both into ecstasy, pounding into Aneurin's body and digging his fingers into Aneurin's hips with every downstroke. Jack filled his body, grunting and seemingly seeking depths he'd never plumbed.

They stayed where they were, panting and recovering, until one by one they separated. Aneurin blessed the generous width of the bed that held them all, though there was little room to spare.

Remo cuddled beside Aneurin on his right, and Jack wearily took his dragon into his arms on Aneurin's left. Aneurin sighed contentedly, grateful to be in the middle where he'd be warmest.

Jack's sleepy and irreverent voice sounded unnaturally loud in the silence. "Welcome to the Royal Academy, gentlemen."

Dragon's Quest
Lena Austin

"Do not meddle in the affairs of dragons..."

The Elf Remo and the spy Quenton are former lovers on opposing missions. Remo must protect the new prince, and Quenton is there to assassinate any human who bonds with the Dragon's Stone as Prince Jack has done. In politics all is deception, and when ugly truths are revealed, who will end up quick-fried to a crackly crunch?

Chapter One

The morning sun, barely risen above the mountaintops outside their school, awakened the Elf Remo after a night of bedsport with the human and the dragon.

Humans. What a delightful race they were, but dragons were definitely better. Remo's ass felt delightfully sore from the attentions of the dragon, Aneurin. He assumed the snores assaulting his pointed ears came from that same dragon, though they could have easily come from the human prince, Jack. The bonded pair of wizard prince and his dragon had been most kind to accept an Elf into their bed, but it was time for Remo to rise as his bladder demanded.

Remo rolled off the bed and stopped short with a smothered groan when he realized his hair was caught beneath the shoulder of Aneurin's slumbering human form. Remo bit his lip and eased it out from beneath the dragon, praying he would awaken neither of his temporary bed partners. His bladder pained him insistently, and though the idea of using the human privy sickened him, Remo stepped into the alcove and pretended he was watering a tree. Elves just didn't belong in huge, damp, musty castles.

Much relieved, Remo dressed and fished the book on humans from his pack to study more of this race he was to envoy to. What he read did not match in the slightest his observations. Where were the greed and discourtesy, the brutishness? Last night had been a delight, full of the courtesies and pleasures one normally only found among Elf-kin. Had Remo missed something in his studies of non-Elven races?

Prince Jack awakened and sat up, groaning at the sunlight streaming in from his window seat. He slid carefully from the bed, his stiff cock pointed at the ceiling, plainly betraying the same need that had awakened Remo. He looked about in confusion, clearly unaware of the privy.

Remo pointed to the alcove and grinned when Jack fled. There would be no further study in his book today, so the Elf laid a tooled leather ribbon to mark his place and waited with curiosity. His studies of non-Elven races had been his downfall, but Remo could not help being fascinated by the clever, lumbering humans.

The human wizard currently under his observation returned from the alcove with a grateful but slightly embarrassed look upon his mobile face. He opened his mouth to speak, but before he could do so, the air shimmered.

The servant who tended their room manifested into view as a simulacrum. The vague form wavered and bowed. "Good morning, my lords. Early morning classes have been cancelled. You and your fellow students are free to socialize. The headmistress has been called to the capital, and will give her welcoming speech at tonight's meal in the dining hall. You will find your afternoon classes listed upon the column at the end of the corridor."

"Thanks, Casper." Prince Jack seemed at ease with the ghostly image, more than many humans might be according to the book, causing Remo additional puzzlement. "Where are the bathrooms, pal? I need a shower."

Casper turned to mist and then solidified. "You make me laugh, Master Jack. The bathhouse resides just before the stables and after the kitchen." He faded from view.

"So that's what it looks like when a simulacrum laughs, huh? Pretty cool." Jack wandered to the bed and slapped Aneurin's ass. "Come on, scaly butt. Let's get clean."

Remo jerked, fully expecting to see the royal heir singed at minimum. He would never have dared awaken his love in such a fashion. Embarrassed, Remo turned to braid his hair to keep it neat.

Aneurin flipped over and upright, with his black hair falling over one sleepy eye. He rubbed his buttocks. "You take unfair advantage of me, Jack. What has made you so cheerful, considering I smell none of that vile coffee you and my mother enjoy so much?"

Jack paused in the middle of pulling on his odd blue trews. "Hmm. I don't know. I feel great, like I downed a whole pot of espresso, with a hearty breakfast on the side. That's odd. I should be starving. We skipped dinner last night in lieu of our horizontal tango."

The Elf snorted. "Foolish wizard. Your body is full of magic, not food. You have glowed with power since you chose the rock at the Trial." Remo stopped to find his thong to tie the end of his braid. "You must eat, and soon, or you will grow as thin as your dragon and die."

Aneurin sucked in his breath and hastened to rise and dress.

Jack blinked in astonishment and knelt on the ground to rummage beneath the chair for one of his odd white boots. "Hmph. I didn't know I could die from wizardry. That's odd. In the dark under this chair, I do glow. Weird. Why aren't you glowing, Remo?"

Remo politely handed Aneurin his jerkin from the floor. The Elf dared not reveal all, but the prince's innocent honesty compelled Remo to answer as truthfully as possible. "I chose an object of lesser power, a small dagger. Your stone radiated much more, like the sun. I'm surprised the others missed it." Remo strangled on his next words, fearful to say the name. "Especially Quenton."

Aneurin snorted and pulled on his boot. "He smelled of garlic, as if he'd bathed in it."

Remo bit his lip. As much as he wished to defend Quenton, the Elf knew he must not. Quenton had been foolish to try to send Remo home, and then revealed Remo's nature as if it were a crime. The Elf sighed and hid his private pain. Quenton could not know Remo was an exile and could never go home again. The Elf also knew why he'd bathed in garlic, but it was not his place to say why.

Remo changed the subject. "I saw your dragon form, Jack. After the Trial, I needed to spend but one last bit of time in the open air before shutting myself in this -- forgive me -- dark place. I lingered in a tree, and saw Aneurin in the sky with a black dragon. I knew it had to be you, transformed. Congratulations."

Jack's jaw fell open and he held the white boot poised over his foot. "Uh, well, I'm not sure… well, I think I did it by accident."

Aneurin nodded his agreement.

Remo was so disappointed his ears drooped. "What a shame. I was hoping you'd impart a little wisdom so I might learn to transform more easily. I'd prefer a winged form myself, but I will be content with what I can manage, even if it is little more than a sparrow."

Jack's eyes narrowed. "By the way, nice subject change. Why do I get the impression both of you want to make me into a mushroom, keep me in the dark, and feed me nothing but bullshit?"

Aneurin jumped up and announced, "I'm starved. Let's eat before you start grilling us."

Thoroughly confused, Remo's glance darted between the human and the dragon. "Mushrooms? Grilling?"

Jack opened the door and waited for them to leave. He bent and muttered in Remo's ear. "I know you and Aneurin are hiding information from me. I want you to tell me the truth."

Remo looked up into those oddly dark moss eyes of Jack's. The Elf monarch got that same look in his eyes when he would not be denied. Remo nodded, feeling much like a rabbit in the jaws of a wolf, though the human had no way of knowing this rabbit had sharp claws. "Very well, then. Perhaps you will allow them to take our food out into the sunlight and air while I tell you what I know?" Remo waited for his nod. "Your dragon's secrets are his own. Those, you must pry from him." The Elf turned and walked with as much dignity as he could muster toward the stairs.

The scents of breakfast wafted up, teasing like a whore. Their mouths watered. They studied the schedule, posted on a column, and to his shame, envy twisted within Remo. "Shifting and transfiguration, then you have flight lessons. I will have swordplay."

Oblivious to Remo's misery, Jack relaxed and clapped Aneurin on the shoulder. "I'll look forward to lessons with DeAngelo."

Finding the dining hall was easy with the noise of many men shouting and laughing. They each took what they wished from the serving tables and fled the assault on their ears. A bench under an oak provided all they needed.

Aneurin and Remo sat upon the grass, while Jack made himself comfortable on the bench. Remo was amused to note how he and Aneurin took the supplicant positions, with their heads lower than the prince.

Jack bit into his meat-stuffed bread roll and raised an eyebrow at Remo.

The Elf took this as a signal to begin and took a deep breath. "I meant no true deception, Prince Jack." Remo smiled thinly at his gasp. "Yes, we -- the Elves -- are aware of who you truly are. Be at peace. We do not mean to expose you to danger. Part of my presence here is to act as your protection, now that we are sure you are not like your sire."

Jack's teeth ground together and his brow creased. "No, I'm nothing like him, and I don't want to be heir. Or king."

Aneurin hissed a warning. In Remo's opinion, Aneurin's bonded had spoken a bit too loudly.

Remo smiled a bit. "That is to your credit." He paused, not sure how to word his reassurances. Prince Jack was likeable and good-hearted. He did not deserve to be kept ignorant, but Remo could not reveal all. "I do not think you will be forced to ascend the throne, if that provides your heart with ease."

The wizard prince drew a shaky breath. His growl was almost inaudible. "Unless you Elves have a spare human royal heir lying around somewhere, I'm sort of stuck with the job."

There was no way to answer that, so they finished their meal in silence, for it seemed Prince Jack had lost his appetite for questions.

Jack regained enough aplomb to thank Remo for his guardianship and the Elves' interest in him while they bathed. Then he seemed to forget his despair. The Elf breathed a sigh of relief while Jack simmered with energy and barely contained excitement as they straggled into one of the many cavernous rooms on the second floor of the mountain castle. His leather robe, worn like a long black coat, matched the rest of his oddly elegant clothes.

Quenton sneered when they entered the classroom, as befitting one who had worn Elf-made silk and woven cloths all his life, but Remo thought Jack's use of the peasant fabric was striking. Without meaning to do so, the prince might start new fashions among the males at the palace. The females indulged themselves shamelessly, but the males resembled bedraggled peahens.

The teacher certainly noticed his beauty. She all but panted with heat like a werewolf female, though even the Elf knew this was one of the ladies of the court. She swallowed and rapped her wand sharply on the table before her.

Aneurin leaned over to tease his bonded with a hurried whisper but loud enough for Remo to hear. "Shall we bet how fast that one enquires of your mother when you will be put to stud?" He earned a sharp jab in his ribs for his sense of humor.

"I am Lady Vera. Every day after luncheon, you will come here to learn to shift both yourself and other creatures, if you have the skills for it. Some of you will not, and this is no shame upon you." She beamed down benevolently, her brown curls nodding in time to her words. "Should you be unable, you will have this time period free, but do not think you may take your ease the rest of the day, for the next hour is spell casting class with Lady Tilda. You will be expected to appear then."

She glanced around the room sternly, but avoided looking at Jack. "Now! Who can shift besides the dragon companions?"

A few raised their hands. Jack did not. Instead he folded his arms across his chest. When Jack saw Remo's raised eyebrow, he muttered, "It's not under my control. I'll work on it."

Lady Vera had sharp ears. "What form do you take, Lord Jack, if you please?"

"A black dragon."

"Well, then. You shall practice in the back of the room. Try not to break anything." She pointed with her wand to a distant corner behind her and lit the mage lamp over that area.

Jack and Aneurin removed themselves to the area indicated. Remo dared not turn his head to watch, though the occasional whiff of sulfur and some vile acidic smell floated toward them.

Lady Vera's lesson was not very useful. "Visualization is the key. You must see from the eyes of the form you wish to be and your mind must see this clearly. Want that form with all your hearts. See it, feel it, and become it." Her eyes strayed to the back of the room, and her eyes widened. "If you please, Lord Jack! If you are going to spread your wings, be kind enough to mind the tapestries."

Remo understood why she spread them around the room soon enough, as almost everyone wanted a large winged form. Quenton taunted Remo by taking the place directly opposite the Elf. Of course, he manifested as a dragon, just as Remo knew he would. His sleek, young, green form, with silver accents, earned him commendations from Lady Vera. She immediately made Quenton her assistant to aid those of the students who experienced difficulties.

The Elf redoubled his efforts, but could not manage the trick of it, only managing to puff out in feathers like a molting chicken. Remo hung his head in shame and closed his eyes. He did not need the scent of garlic in his nose to know that Quenton was beside him.

Quenton's breath teased his ears. In Remo's own language, he uttered reassurances. "Do not fear me, Remo. I would not be so cruel here." He placed one hand on Remo's back. "Stop fighting what you really want to be. You know what it is. Take it."

Remo looked up. There was much to be said they dared not. The Elf saw naked lust in his dark eyes. "Do you really want me to take what I want?"

Quenton's hand moved lower. "Why not? I certainly intend to."

* * *

Remo trembled like a leaf in a high wind, but refused to acknowledge the hand now resting just a finger's width from his ass. His skin flushed with heat, and he was sure his breathing quickened. What was the hold Quenton had on his heart? He lifted his chin and looked into the stormy darkness of Quenton's eyes. "We are not lovers anymore, Quenton. I have not given you permission to touch my body."

The brown eyes he'd once loved softened, and Quenton looked away. "You know why I left. I was as frightened as you of loving one not of my own race, though it's more acceptable among my kind than yours. We were too young, Remo."

Remo sighed and softened his voice. "Did you think the passage of time would make a difference?" His lips twisted into a half-smile at the irony of it all. "You've been consorting with humans too long. Marking the passage of time is a human trait."

Quenton's lip curled into a snarl. "I have my duties to my queen. I do what I must."

"Temperamental as always, I see." Remo winged an eyebrow upward and ignored the soaring lust in his groin. No one had ever stirred his heart -- and shattered it -- as Quenton had and still could. "At least I am honest in why I am here."

His ex-lover chuckled. "Liar. What would they say if they knew who and what you really are, Remo? Would they call you spy and send your lovely head back to your king?" He leaned closer. "It would be such a waste when I'd rather be fucking that sweet mouth of yours once more."

Lust and rage hazed Remo's vision until he could barely see. His ragged breaths sounded harsh to his own ears while the rest of the world faded away to shadows. Worst of all, his mouth watered at the memories of doing precisely what Quenton described. Days spent in a tangle of flesh together. "You demean my honor. I have not lied."

Quenton removed his hand from Remo's ass and stepped back one pace. In a low, insinuating tone, he accused Remo of pure dishonor. "A lie of omission is still a lie. You haven't told the whole truth, have you?"

Mage energy crackled between them. Quenton allowed it to travel up his body and be absorbed. His eyes lit and for a brief moment turned golden. He hissed, "Do it, Remo. Change and fight me on my own turf. Become a danger to me."

A red mist hazed Remo's vision, seemingly coloring the whole world in blood. Remo gave one inarticulate scream of pure rage. He leapt at Quenton, not sure if he would kill or kiss, but something -- anything -- was better than standing still one moment longer. His wings buffeted Quenton, and his tail lifted to sting that self-satisfied smirk... Wait... His wings? His tail?

Shouts penetrated his confusion. "Holy Mother! A wyvern!" "Did you see that? Remo turned into a wyvern." "Someone rescue Quenton before Remo stings him to death!"

Quenton fell bonelessly to the flagstones, out cold from the force of Remo's wings. One of Remo's talons was snagged on his jerkin, so perforce Remo went down with his former lover. Remo's wyvern shriek of surprise and confusion echoed and bounced off the walls.

A purple wing interposed itself between the two of them and the rest of the students. The golden eyes of a dragon softened sympathetically, and winked reassurance.

"Easy there, Remo." Prince Jack edged around the wing, moving slowly with his hands outstretched. "Calm down, pal. I want to help."

Help? Oh, yes, he needed help. His wings stopped their agitated flapping, and the tension in his tail relaxed, uncurling until it lay flat upon the floor. Remo watched his tail -- with the wicked-looking stinger dripping poison -- in fascination.

Prince Jack moved closer, daring to kneel within easy strike range of Remo's deadly appendage. "Remo, look at me. I'm going to untangle your claw from Quenton's vest. Don't bite me, okay?"

The other students peered around Aneurin's wing, for surely the purple wing belonged to Jack's dragon. One pronounced in an awed tone, "Gods. Does he know what he's risking?"

Remo hissed at that remark, and they all stepped back a pace. A distant tugging distracted Remo, and he angled his long neck to see Jack working each individual claw out from the lacings of Quenton's silk jerkin.

Quenton moaned and opened the one eye that wasn't going to be swollen shut within a matter of hours. He reached one hand up feebly to caress Remo's pointed muzzle. "That was worth every bruise and ache. Congratulations."

Jack grunted and freed the last talon from Quenton's clothes. "You pissed him off to make him change? That could have gotten you killed, dimwit."

Quenton shrugged. "It was that or make him burst with lust. This was neither the time nor place for lovemaking. I had to risk his anger instead."

Remo kept his thoughts to himself. He doubted his stinger would have done more than make Quenton sick, though it might have killed anyone else in the room. He blinked innocently and tried to remain calm. Wyverns were notoriously irascible creatures, inclined to sting first and not bother to ask questions.

Jack moved slowly away from Quenton's supine body, careful not to startle Remo. He spoke gently and carefully. "Okay, Remo. Back up and allow Quenton to rise. He'll pay for annoying you with a lot of pain tonight. Easy now. Use your tail for balance. Remember, you only have two legs and wings right now. Careful."

Remo discovered "walk" was not part of a wyvern's abilities. His legs responded more like an eagle's, making it possible for him to hop, or move in an ungainly sidestepping motion forward. He settled for hopping a few feet backwards.

As soon as Remo was safely away, Jack moved forward to help Quenton sit up. "Anything broken?"

Quenton smiled, despite a cut lip. "Not even my pride. My thanks." He allowed Jack to haul him by one arm to his feet. Quenton turned and bowed to Remo. "When you calm down, you should be able to return to your Elven shape. Perhaps I can repay the debt of my insults with a glass of Elven wine? I shall owe you and your dragon a glass of wine as well, Lord Jack, for you were the only ones brave enough to risk a painful death to save me. Again, my thanks."

Aneurin quietly furled his wings and allowed Quenton to exit into the crowd of students, who followed him out the door murmuring like a pack of love struck maidens.

Lady Vera stepped forward, her hands on her hips, and shook her head at the exiting men. She sniffed derisively and then turned to nod at Jack. "I am most impressed, Lord Jack. You show the bravery of your aunts. I will see to it you are excused from Lord DeAngelo's classes, if you wish it."

Jack bowed. "I doubt that will be necessary, Lady Vera. Remo will calm down now that Quenton is removed from his sight, I'm sure."

"Foolish thing to do. Never anger another mage until you know their full abilities. I shall speak to him once his bruises ache sufficiently to drive home the lesson." She gathered up her skirts and swept from the room.

Jack muttered in the direction of the door. "Actually, it's not bravery. I have no idea what wyverns can do." He cleared his throat and looked nervously at Remo's stinger. "Let me guess. That thing's poisonous, right?"

Laughter bubbled up inside Remo, at first coming out like a raucous high-pitched screech before settling into normal tones as his sense of humor facilitated his return to his usual Elven form. "You are much too innocent for your own good, Jack."

Grinning with relief, Jack snorted. "First time anyone's told me that."

Aneurin chimed in. "Well, you said you wanted a form with wings. You got one." He eyed the tiny iridescent puddle of poisoned ichor where Remo's tail had been. "With one helluva weapon included in the bargain."

Remo sighed. "It is a saying among my people. Be careful what you wish for. The gods have a sense of humor."

Chapter Two

Quenton kept his chin up and his back straight while the sycophants chattered like magpies, commending his bravery and expressing their concern over his injuries. His head ached abominably, he could only see out of one eye, and he'd be black and blue in the morning judging by the way his muscles protested every movement. Still, he couldn't help smiling in satisfaction. He'd mended the breach between himself and Remo, and possibly redeemed himself in Prince Jack's eyes. His mission might yet succeed, if he could ally himself with the two most powerful wizards in the castle. If he'd manipulated the situation as well as he'd hoped, he'd also relieve the ache in his groin by sunrise. One could always hope.

The swordmaster's salle and fighting field was a long, painful walk but well worth the journey. His muscles wouldn't stiffen and they'd be properly warmed for swordplay. Lord Damek scared the whey out of the fools around Quenton, and they'd be silent, thank the Mother. He breathed a sigh of relief to see the husky, muscular warrior lounging in the sun on the bench outside the salle.

The gruff swordmaster studied Quenton's black eye. "Fighting already? One might think you were boys, not men who should control themselves." He scanned the crowd surrounding Quenton. "Well? What are you waiting for? An invitation from the king? Armor up! Move." They scattered like geese.

Quenton turned to follow, but with dignity. The swordmaster's hand on his right biceps stopped him. He swallowed a wince when the bruise twinged.

"Who were you fighting with, Lord Quenton?"

Proudly, Quenton lifted his chin. "It wasn't a fight precisely, Lord Damek. I angered the Elf Remo to force him to transfigure. It worked, but I shall pay for my methods."

Damek's eyes lifted and looked over Quenton's shoulder. Not that Quenton needed the hint. He'd felt Remo approach, for once alone. Prince Jack and his dragon would be at flight practice with that insane old wizard.

The swordmaster grunted once, his eyes still trained on Remo. "Remo, do you sword fight by the usual Elven methods?" Damek did not release Quenton's arm.

Quenton turned in time to see Remo bow. "Indeed, good swordmaster. I do."

The other students trooped out of the salle wearing various combinations of armor and weapons, according to their preferences and skills.

Another grunt. "Well and good then. I'll have no ill feelings between my students." The swordmaster studied the crowd with no pity. "You're not all that handsome a lot, most of you, but I remind you that you're all certified wizards and therefore at stud when requested. You can't do your duty when you're damaged goods." He grabbed Quenton's chin and jerked him around until all could get a good look at the blackened and rapidly swelling eye, then just as rapidly released Quenton entirely.

The students shuffled their feet, some with their faces as red as peonies.

Lord Damek snorted. "Virgins. Get over it. Lord Kyle will see to your training in pleasuring the ladies who hire you. That's not my job. My job is to see to it your wizard skills are up to the task of serving as warlocks in battle and that means learning to defend yourselves first. Can't have you being killed. Just try not to damage your ugly faces any more than you have to."

The students looked at one another, some grinning, some thoughtful.

Quenton moved to stand with the others, only a few feet from Remo, just to watch the Elf flush. Remo was in the same state he was, nearly bursting with lust. It radiated off him in red waves. Quenton suppressed a smile of satisfaction.

Damek wasn't finished. He pointed at Remo and Quenton. "You and you. Pair up. Work out any ill will between you with blunted practice weapons. No rules. You may use the wooded area as well as that space." He pointed to a round dueling circle. "I'll grant the Elf will need a forest to use his skills. Return the blades and armor by sunset. Go."

Quenton turned and marched into the salle without a word. He chose his weapon, an imitation of a hand-and-a-half broadsword, and shrugged on a lightly padded gambeson.

Remo, in the manner of his people, chose a thin, light sword and a similarly padded vest.

As one, they stalked outside, shoulder to shoulder, ignoring the crowd now spread about the field under the supervision of Lord Damek. Lord Damek's insults as to their clumsiness and "dancing" peppered the air.

They took positions in the dueling circle, saluted, and warily began to circle one another, as they had done many times before.

Quenton couldn't repress his grin any longer. "Just like old times, eh, Remo?"

Remo made the opening move and danced away from the parry. "Not at all."

"I wish it were." Quenton returned a strike, moving with all the speed he could muster. He clipped Remo's shoulder, but once more the Elf escaped with nothing more than a touch.

"If wishes were dragons, we all could ride." Remo tossed back his braid and wove a complicated pattern with his blade.

Quenton laughed. There was the opening he'd waited for. He rushed Remo to break the woven pattern of the sword dance. "You can ride me anytime and you know it."

Remo stepped backward, until he stood just inside the ring of trees marking the edge of the woods. He snorted once and stepped into the shadows. "I know it."

Quenton raced after him. "Then let the chase begin."

* * *

Remo blended into a clump of bushes, and squatted down to hide for a moment. The scent of the earth, normally so soothing, did not still his beating heart. He heard Quenton crash through the foliage, intent on pursuit. Remo put his head in his hands and swallowed a moan. What was he doing? One did not tease a dragon without risking a burn, as the humans said, but teasing Quenton was doubly foolish. They risked both their missions.

"I can smell you, Remo," Quenton's voice coaxed. "I know you're nearby. What do you fear from me?" The dark-haired wizard stalked right by Remo's hiding place. It wouldn't be long before he sniffed out his Elven prey, damn his superior senses.

Failure. Success. That's what I fear. Remo shuddered, admitting to himself he wanted to be back in Quenton's arms, damn their separate goals. He ached for Quenton's lips on his body, to taste Quenton's sweet cock in his mouth before they fucked each other into oblivion.

Quenton sniffed loudly. "I can smell your lust, my Elven lover. Why do you hide?" He turned, tasting the air without changing to his true form. "You know I won't hurt you."

That was true. Remo studied Quenton's strong, muscular back, his gaze trailing down to the well-sculpted buttocks of one who took his part of a human lordling seriously. Had Quenton been playing his role all the time they'd been apart? What was his mission here that his queen had sent him to do?

Quenton's face turned up to gauge the time by the sun's position. "We have only a few hours until sunset, Remo. Would you have me chase you or spend this interlude in pleasure?"

The temptation was too great. Remo had to ask. He sighed and stood, smiling slightly. Soundlessly, he moved as only a forest dweller could, and then raked his hand between Quenton's butt cheeks. His grin widened when the dark wizard yelped and spun in midair. "And what of afterward, lover? Will we return to our separate duties, waiting until we have prevented this race war to be together again?"

Quenton gathered his smaller lover into his arms with tenderness. He buried his face in Remo's neck. "Right now, I am too impatient to care what becomes of tomorrow. Why can we not just be as we once were?"

Remo squirmed in delight as Quenton's dark curls tickled his sensitive ear tips. His mind fogged like an autumn meadow on a misty morning, with Quenton's hardness poking insistently through his light Elven vest. "We are older now, that's why. No longer can we run off into the woods like naughty younglings to play. We… oh, spirits of air… stop that. I can't think."

"Good. I don't want you to think. I want you to feel." Quenton lifted his lips from Remo's ear, where he'd been diligently flicking his tongue just inside the shell. His arms, still wrapped around Remo, lifted the Elf off the ground as if he were a feather. "Come here. I will do now what I didn't know was needed then. I will seduce my bright star into flaming for me."

The last of Remo's resistance crumbled. Of their own accord, Remo's legs wound around Quenton's hips. The barrier he kept around his heart, allowing only light love affairs, cracked and shook. "You haven't called me that in a very long time."

"Wait one moment. You'll harm yourself on my sword belt. Let me remove it, I beg." Quenton's voice was thick with emotion. It gratified Remo to know he was not the only one in danger of losing all discretion.

"Remove it all or remove me from your arms, but be quick about it."

"As you wish." Quenton lifted Remo out of his arms and placed him on a low tree stump where Remo could be eye to eye with his taller lover. "I will not risk magic. There are too many here who would recognize my spell. You must watch me strip away these human clothes one by one."

"To the darkest dwarven halls with that. No one knows Elven magic." Remo swept away their clothes with a wave of his hand. Their clothes landed in piles at the base of the tree. "We'll sort them later." He wriggled forward, prepared to jump down and join Quenton on the soft, springy grass.

Quenton's hands grasped Remo's thighs and held him in place. "Nay, do not be so anxious. We have an hour or two as yet, and I've dreamt of tasting your honey sweet flesh so often, I wish to sup and savor."

"Oh." Remo bent forward, his lips hovering above Quenton's, torturing them both with anticipation. "Well then, I admit I dreamt likewise. These first, I think."

A growl tore from Quenton's throat. His hand tangled in the braid at the back of Remo's neck and he yanked the Elf forward. "Who said I would permit you to be in charge?"

Quenton took Remo's mouth with his own, a silent dare to Remo to stop him. Fortunately, such a halt was far from Remo's plans. He parted his lips and let Quenton's long tongue taste what they'd both denied themselves for far too long. He wanted to swallow Quenton whole, devouring… oh, wait… that would be Quenton's thoughts, merging with his own. He shoved them aside, determined to keep his soul-self separate.

Chuckling, Quenton released Remo's lips. "One day, you'll let me in all the way, Remo. I want more than your body, and I always have. Now I'm just less afraid to take what I want."

Remo shook his finger at his lover's long, elegant nose. "Take what I give and be grateful. If you think you can simply saunter back into my life and body after well over one hundred years, you are sadly mistaken."

"Now who's counting time?" Quenton's eyes glittered with mischief.

Stammering was not elegant, but Remo choked when he realized he had indeed marked the passage of the years. "I could not help but notice." He looked into the dark, earth-brown eyes he loved and softened his voice to a bare whisper. "I missed you so."

Quenton's hands grasped Remo's arms and yanked him off the tree stump. He crushed Remo to his chest, sheer happiness lighting his face. "And I could not live one day without thinking of you, wondering who shared your bed in my place, and if you would ever forgive me for running like a scared rabbit."

"Oh, I think I can manage a bit of mercy." Remo's eyes glittered with mischief, and his heart was lighter than it had been in many decades. "Perhaps if you could satiate us both before the sun sets, this might ease the way?"

"Oh, I do love a challenge. They're irresistible to me." Quenton gently put Remo down atop some thick moss growing between two tree roots. "Here's a fine bed to lay the most beautiful Elf in Honalee."

Remo snorted, mildly insulted. He ignored the cool moss that would stain his silver hair to green. "Females are beautiful. Males are handsome. I remind you that for all that I'm smaller than you, I am not weaker."

Quenton knelt next to Remo, his appreciative gaze warmer than the sun filtering through the trees. "I know this quite well. Your king was wise to send one who is fond of other races, but yet is powerful and clever enough to do battle." He bent to taste one of Remo's nipples, his teeth nipping just at the point of pain.

The Elf buried his hands in his lover's familiar curls, savoring the long remembered feel. His heart soared higher than eagles… or dragons. "Exile among humans was a fate worse than death."

Quenton's eyes were large and round when his gaze lifted from Remo's body. "Exile? How dare they?"

Blushing at having revealed too much, Remo lifted his heels. His body shook with both embarrassment and need. Fortunately, it was easy to distract his lover's emotional outbursts. "We will discuss it later over that wine you owe me."

Fire heated the large dark eyes he so loved. "Don't think I'll forget. I, too, am older, and my memory more refined. But for the moment I will permit an interlude of mystery. Meanwhile --" and in his hand appeared a small flagon of oil, "-- we shall indulge ourselves."

"Good. I began to wonder if you expected me to provide the oil you intended to fuck me into forgetfulness with." Remo knew his eyes flashed with heat equal to his lover's.

Quenton chuckled and lavished the oil upon his cock, teasing Remo by slathering it inch by inch with the glistening lubricant. "This will ease my way, though I admit I considered doing without when you dismissed me so blithely before the Trials." He pressed into Remo's body, sliding slowly home. Even after so long, he fit as a sword in its own scabbard.

Remo cried out in joy and sensation. Quenton's cock filled him and completed his soul, with pleasure and pain so intricately mixed, they became a wicked dichotomy. Too long had it been since he'd felt so full, locked in his one true love's embrace.

Quenton's face mirrored his own passions, but perhaps he had learned patience and consideration, because he chose to stay still and allow Remo's body a chance to adjust to the intrusion. Instead, he used his oily right hand to grasp Remo's cock and stroke it. "We will come together in our own good time, lover Elf."

The double entendre did not escape Remo, despite the dual pleasures that had him writhing beneath Quenton. He wasn't sure what to focus on -- the tug and pull on his aching length or the stretch and pull of his full ass. To do what Quenton asked was so very tempting, so very easy. *Just relax and let it happen.* If only he dared risk his heart again. One word hissed from him. "Perhaps."

"From you, that is concession enough you admit it could happen. I can be patient, for I've learned to wait for my forest lover." Quenton pulled out and pushed Remo's legs until they slid beneath the lordling's arms. Effortlessly, he leaned backwards, lifted Remo on his lap, sitting simultaneously on his own heels and balancing his lover there. "Ride me this way, then."

Happily impaled once more, Remo rode, using Quenton's broad shoulders to lever himself up and down, pushing Quenton's cock deep within. He could have died of the pleasure, for Quenton's hand had returned to teasing his cock to screaming life. Could a near-immortal Elf die of such ecstasy? Perhaps. He didn't care anymore. "I bless your queen for sending you to protect the young prince. I'll send her one of my best jewels for her collection."

Quenton's free left hand pinched the Elf's pale nipple, but Quenton's face twisted with the effort of holding back his full passions. His true voice grated out in a growl. "Not here for that."

The surprise was enough to distract Remo from the dichotomy of the two different sensations, and he threw his head back as their passion merged into a seamless whole. His body flared, signaling impending release.

Quenton roared and his hands grasped Remo's waist to pull him up and plunge him down, hard and fast, impaling his Elf lover deeply in their joining.

With their shared release, Remo's soul soared without wings to the sun, as Quenton had always done for him before -- giving him wings when he had none of his own. He'd longed to fly, and now Quenton had given him that, too, risking his own life.

The years fell away, and the trust returned, more precious than love itself. His heart and mind opened and allowed Quenton reentrance. The whirlwind of shared emotion and experience came flooding in, never to be sundered until death.

Still now, with the juice of Remo's ecstasy between them, they paused and allowed the bond to finish it. Remo leaned in and allowed his head to rest against Quenton's forehead. Between their harsh, panted breaths, an image floated to the surface of Quenton's mind.

Remo blinked. He knew that image. Had he not seen it the day before? "Why does that odd rock Prince Jack chose in the Trials hold your attention when you should be thinking only of me?"

His teasing words brought a startled jerk from Quenton. His bond mate's strong arms painfully latched on to Remo's biceps. "What do you mean?"

Despite the bruising, Quenton's intense question was more than startling to Remo. He wondered at the shock in Quenton's eyes. "Didn't you see the stone? You were tested before Prince Jack."

Through their shared link, Quenton absorbed the scene of Jack moving about the table, hand out to test mage currents, and eyes shut to minimize distraction. Then Quenton saw in Remo's mind the detail even the Elf mage had missed. An ordinary stone charged with mage energy flared and was exchanged for… "No. I don't believe this." He released Remo, setting his bonded love aside, and put his face in his hands.

Remo recognized his distress, not only from the miserable picture before him, but from the horror that echoed through their shared bond. He kissed and petted his lover, coaxing Quenton to share. "Why do you worry so about a rock?"

Quenton did not lift his head. "That was no ordinary rock, my lover Elf. That was the Dragon's Stone, and it has done what was only legend before now. It has chosen a human to bond with."

Slowly, Remo's jaw drifted downward. "But, but, we thought the human king stole it."

"He did. And now his son has bonded with it. Prince Jack now controls the entire dragon race if he so chooses."

Chapter Three

"Prince Jack must die." The utter despair of voicing those words made even Quenton wince. By all the commands issued by his beloved Queen, his orders were clear -- allow no human to control all dragon kind. Never before had his duties caused him one second's thought. Now he felt his bile rise, and he choked.

Remo clutched his arms, shivering. "No, Quenton. You must not! Prince Jack is not like his father! This I would swear before your queen and my king both." His lips twitched. "He is perhaps the most innocent of humans, and certainly of nobles, that I've ever seen. Most endearing, actually. Even if he never ascends to the throne, he does not deserve to die."

Quenton lifted bleak eyes to Remo. His gut wrenched, and he held his Elf close, both to warm him and to promise love. Above all else, he would not destroy the fragile bond they'd forged that very hour. "Do you say this because you are charged with guarding his life?"

A mock slap on his cheek, barely enough to sting, answered. "Come! We have played assassin many times, but always upon a deserving culprit. We merely arranged their meeting with the Creative Force a bit sooner than fated. When have we ever felt sorrow for our target? The fact that we do feel it is wrong to harm Prince Jack is warning enough."

Quenton looked up, wishing and hoping for an answer from the Queen of Heaven. The fading light through the trees gave him a chance to seek a way to stay his hand. Quenton took the excuse of the setting sun like a gift. He would think. Jack need not die tonight. "Our time alone is over, my little love. We must dress before the weapons master seeks us and we give him cause to blush."

Remo nodded and squirmed lithely off Quenton's lap. He fetched their clothes and tossed Quenton's beside him. Quickly, he dressed and picked up his sword.

Wordlessly, Quenton slid into the hated human clothing, and longed for the freedom of nothing between his body and the air. The night was chill, and this frail human form felt the cold rising like an accursed fog. He tried for a bit of humor, hoping to bring back the joy of their bonding. "I think we may honestly tell the weapons master that we have fully reconciled our differences."

The Elf snorted, his eyes twinkling with humor. "Indeed. I agree with that statement. Though in the interval since he saw us last, you have grown much the worse for wear. Are you in pain?"

Quenton blinked, and assessed his injuries. Yes, his eye hurt and a few muscles twanged, but now he had the nearly unlimited power of an Elf mage to draw upon. He would be fine in the morning. "Nothing that would cause me to lose sleep. I'll be nearly healed by morning."

Woods-wise as his race's reputation claimed, Remo sniffed the breeze once and sure-footedly led the way back to the dueling circle. "Of course. I can feel you drawing on me."

"Only fair, since you caused these injuries." Quenton suppressed the pride he felt in having given his love his fondest wish -- wings to fly.

Lord Damek waited with folded arms in the center of the dueling circle. The last of their fellow students, looking sweat-soaked, trudged toward the castle. He grunted to see them both disheveled, with moss and bark in their hair. "Good. You made it rough on each other. I declare Remo the winner, since he looks barely touched, and you look like twenty leagues of bad road. Get on to the castle for your suppers. Quenton, mind you visit the herbalist for a poultice for that eye after dinner."

As soon as they were out of earshot, Remo pretended to stumble so he came closer to Quenton than normally allowed. "I'd best not be seen with you. A public enmity suits me for now." He grasped Quenton's arm and pulled himself upright. "Don't make me harm you to protect the prince, I beg of you." He then sprinted toward the palace.

Quenton continued his slow, painful walk toward the palace, hoping he'd arrive long after all others had settled in the dining hall. Were it not for his rumbling belly, he'd prefer to barricade himself in his room. His supposed rank had secured him a private room, but that did not guarantee peace.

He scrubbed his one undamaged eye and wished fervently for an end to the masquerade. No, he did not want to kill the prince. He'd admired Jack for rushing to defend one he saw as smaller and weaker, and then for risking a wyvern's sting to rescue one he perceived to be an enemy. Did such humans really still exist? Apparently so.

He swung through the doors of the dining hall as carelessly as he could manage, pretending to be the arrogant lordling once more. The normally noisy room was unusually silent. He bowed to the frowning headmistress, earning himself a curt nod for interrupting her speech.

A servant brought him a platter laden with meat as Lady Tilda continued. His starving state encouraged him to stuff as much as he dared in his mouth without losing the hard-won manners of human nobility.

She fluttered and fumbled with her notes, as if she'd lost her place. "Ahem! As I was saying, His Majesty is most concerned for the students here, especially the dragon mates."

That statement got his attention in a hurry. Quenton looked up, pausing in mid-chew. What about the dragon mates? What had he missed? He glanced over at Jack and Aneurin, the two most notable dragon mates present, though there were a few others as well. They were lovingly sitting shoulder to shoulder, their attention focused on Lady Tilda. Quenton swallowed sheer envy.

Tilda's falsely guileless blue eyes strayed to study each of the dragon pairs in turn. "Yes, this concerns you most of all. It is moving toward fall, when dragons often rise to mate. His Majesty recognizes that this is a natural occurrence, and has given a special dispensation to all the student wizards bonded to a dragon. If your dragon shows distress and the need to rise, all you must do is contact the nearest teacher. A noble lady will avail herself in your rooms to provide you with comfort during that arduous time."

Snickers and outright titters erupted around the room. Good-natured pokes in the arm hit all the grinning human partners of a bonded pair. All except Jack, who had turned white. Quenton didn't blame him.

Tilda sniffed and cleared her throat. "Settle down. Settle down. This is no cause for amusement. I daresay you'll be less amused when a normally placid dragon suddenly becomes irritable enough to cause you injury. Any change in personality or normal behavior is to be reported immediately, in case the dragon needs sequestering."

The dragons barely controlled snarls of outrage. Even Aneurin seemed insulted, and well they all might. One of the female dragons stood up, her fists clenched at her side and her eyes blazing. Her mate tugged her back down beside him and cuddled her close.

Such rubbish. Quenton restrained himself from displaying one iota of the insult that had just been handed down so blithely. Sequestering his bruised ass. Restraint, she meant. As if any dragon would put up with any loss of their freedom, much less a separation from a bond mate.

Remo's worried eyes caught his from across the room. One silver eyebrow lifted in silent question.

Quenton shook his head minutely and speared another piece of meat as if it was no concern of his. He longed to reassure Remo, and more so did he ache to share Remo's bed and warmth. But for this night if no other, Quenton would be alone. He would not sleep in any case.

As Lady Tilda rattled on, listing a ridiculous litany of supposed signs of an impending need to rise that came close to laughable, it dawned on Quenton that the excuse of watching for dragon heat was just that -- an excuse.

Changes in behavior and personality were signs of the Dragon's Stone in use. He stole a glance at Prince Jack, engaged in soothing his outraged dragon. They were trying to ascertain if he'd bonded with the Stone. Quenton would have given his teeth to be certain of that as well.

He had to warn Remo, but their newly awakened mating was too fresh even if he dared try to speak to

Remo's mind across a crowded, noisy room. Anyone with the ability would hear Quenton make the attempt, and his ruse would be up. No, he would have to wait until tomorrow and no help for it.

The meal seemed to last hours, even after Lady Tilda finished her long-winded speech and permitted conversation. The sycophants he'd cultivated chattered inanely, cooing over Quenton's bruises like a bunch of brainless dryads. His dinner soured in his stomach.

Finally, he could take no more. Quenton shoved his chair back and grimaced at the loud scrape. "Forgive me, my friends, but I would like to acquire a poultice for my eye and shroud my aching head in darkness." He bowed politely and swallowed contempt as they simpered like untried maidens. "I shall see you on the morrow, if I am better."

Without waiting for their agreement, he turned and sauntered toward the door that led to the chirugeon's office.

Once out of sight, he fled up the stairs and slipped into his room with a grateful sigh. His friends weren't really that bad for company. He'd chosen them all carefully for their value as information siphons, connections to others, or other reasons that had little to do with true friendships. It was hard to hold a decent conversation when you had so many secrets to hide, but a good conversationalist was one who said little and listened much.

Once, just once, he'd like to have a whole day where he did not have to be anything but what he truly was.

Quenton sighed and pulled out his scrying ball from its leather case. The clarity and size of the crystal was more than most wizards could ever hope to afford, but its true value lay in who it connected to. Quenton knelt before it and keyed the spell that opened a direct communication between himself and his queen. Had he been in his true form, his head would be in the dust before her, but this would do.

"Quenton! What news have you? Have you found the Stone?" The great dragoness hissed and put her golden head forward eagerly. A few of the many gems that made her glittering bed rattled off the pile, to be scooped up by her fire elemental servants and returned carefully to their positions.

"I have not found the Stone, My Queen, but I bear news that is both good and bad." He faltered and choked, knowing his duty but not liking what would happen. "The Stone has chosen a human and, I believe, bonded to him."

The roar, muffled by the crystal, still hurt his ears. "Kill the human. No. Wait. You say there is some good from this?"

"Yes, Mother. I mean, My Queen." Quenton bowed his head hastily, knowing he was but one of the queen's many offspring, and certainly not her favorite. "The chosen human is by all accounts just what the legends say the Stone chooses. He is reported to be kind, intelligent, and wise. What I have seen of him bears this out. Additionally, he does not yet know what has transpired."

A puff of smoke from her nostrils matched her thoughtful snort. "I see." Her golden eyes closed for a moment. "I sense in you a reluctance to kill the human. Why?"

He swallowed, not sure how to answer. "Not only do I feel the human may be what the legends say, but also…" Quenton winced. This was going to hurt. "He's the son of the present Usurper."

Only distance and the muffling spell on the crystal kept the whole castle from hearing her roar. He privately wondered why the crystal did not crack under the strain. The queen's forelegs trampled her nest in her agitation, dislodging so many gems her servants could not gather them all. "By the eggs of our foremothers!"

Quenton waited patiently while she worked out what he'd already had time to consider. The cold of the floor was seeping up through his knees, and he stilled his shivers. If she kept him on his knees until he fell into torpor, so be it. He'd prove himself to be a worthy son, able to do the most difficult task unflinchingly.

Finally, she sank back on her nest. "So. We skim a cliff in a tempest. If we kill the prince, we risk war. If we do not, we risk losing our freedom to his commands." She closed her eyes, weighing all the options. "Very well. I am forced to trust your observations. If you can, ally yourself with the prince, for he may now act as the northern star to guide us to the Stone. We shall test his mettle, and see if he is the stuff of legends."

* * *

She grasped the shaft of meat firmly in her hand, and licked the end just under her nose with loving delicacy. Her tongue flickered into the hole, drinking in the salt-sweet sauce oozing from the core. A tiny bit of cream dribbled down her chin, plopped on the tip of one breast, and slid between her thighs. The males watching her performance followed the progress of the cream avidly. She giggled. "Whoops, I'm feeding everything, aren't I?"

Aneurin jerked and looked accusingly at his lover, Jack. "I thought you said they had no teeth down there!"

Remo's beer spattered across the table while everyone roared with laughter. He'd been totally unprepared for the joke, being preoccupied with his longing for Quenton. In the three days since their tryst in the woods, no other meetings had been possible, and they'd been forced to content themselves with longing looks across the dining hall. But this evening, Quenton had not appeared at all.

Kitiarey put her meat roll on her plate and pretended to be offended. Her lips twitched before she too burst into delighted chuckles. "Aneurin, you are such a jester. That's what I get for teasing, right, my dearest love?" Her large, dark violet eyes turned to her human bond mate.

He cuddled her close and kissed her pert nose. "I think Aneurin has more to fear from your beating him in flight class than if you rose for mating as they so foolishly think you might." He glared balefully at the head table.

Another bonded pair snorted simultaneously, summing up all their feelings about such nonsense, and the chatter soon returned to good-natured banter.

Remo signaled a servant to clean up the spill he'd made and returned to his silent brooding. He'd never felt so cold and alone, even with that tiny warm spot that signaled a dragon bond he dared not acknowledge. Where was Quenton?

He'd fought with himself on whether to warn Jack about Quenton or not. Worse, he could see that Jack had indeed bonded with the Dragon's Stone, though he was completely unaware of this fact. The table full of dragons and their bond mates, attracted by the subtle pull of the Stone's possessor, was proof enough of that. Jack expressed astonishment that they'd want to be seen with the student who could barely manage to remain strapped in his saddle, much less fight or spell cast.

Remo saw no reason to enlighten him. Yet.

A tiny green dragon made of intricately folded paper fluttered like a clumsy butterfly toward them, making straight for Remo. Its delicate little wings flashed with the sparkle of the silverpoint pen and ink used to inscribe the message it carried.

He put out his hand, and the little dragon landed on his palm. The wings lifted once, and then stilled, the magic spent. Remo crushed the paper into a wad and stuffed it into his pouch with no regard for the delicate art that created it.

Jack blinked, plainly a little shocked. "Aren't you going to look to see who sent you an origami dragon?"

Remo shook his head, his lips firmly pressed together. The color of the paper alone told him who sent it. He'd read the rest in private. "What is origami?"

Jack launched into a complicated explanation of the art of folding paper to create animals and shapes as performed by a people with yellow skin and eyes more slanted than an Elf's, but possessing a beautiful and ancient culture. The others leaned forward, fascinated as Jack used a water goblet to create an illusion of his descriptions. He was a lousy rider, but he was a superb wizard, able to translate the "teck-naw-logy" of his adopted world to Honalee.

Remo sat back, smiling, and began to concoct a suitable excuse for disappearing from sight for the evening. The cold little spot in his belly warmed and began to spread at the prospect.

* * *

Quenton breathed a sigh of pure relief when Remo crept silently around the open door of the salle.

His cock hardened immediately at the sight of Remo's moonlight hair vying with the orb in the sky for shine and beauty. Quenton personally felt his Elf won. He knew he was just a besotted dragon in the throes of a new bond, but that didn't matter one whit. "Hello, beautiful." He held out his arms.

The joyous grin on Remo's face did outshine the moon, and he leapt into Quenton's arms with abandon. One fast, hot kiss burned between them. Remo's nose wrinkled for a moment as they broke off. "I can't wait until you stop bathing in garlic to hide your draconic scent from the other dragons."

Quenton chuckled and held his Elf tight, nuzzling the white silk on Remo's head. "I've been grateful they're all bonded and never spent much time in the Lair, or they'd surely recognize my scent."

Remo nibbled on Quenton's collarbone and moved closer. "I cannot wait for this to be over. I want a proper bonding retreat with you somewhere. Perhaps the sea. I've never seen it."

Despite his body responding to his Elf's attentions, Quenton could easily envision long days curled up in the sands, or diving deep for food. "There's a plant that grows on the sea floor. I hear it's delicious. I'd get it for you."

His lover's hand stole up to clench in Quenton's dark curls. Remo's eyes burned with the intensity of his need. "We'll discuss it later. Right now, I want you. Three days was much too long."

"There's a bench over there to throw you over, and I've put a padded gambeson down for your comfort." He suited words to action, half-carrying Remo to the bench. "Whisk our clothes away, my Elf. I'm in a hurry."

"I can see you'll forget how to undress, if you remain impatient for the rest of our days." Yet their clothes vanished, to reappear on another nearby bench. Remo eyed the broken spear and strips of cloth on the floor next to the bench. A slow grin twitched his lips, and his slanted green eyes glowed for a moment. "Going to tie me up, lover?"

Quenton reached down and hefted the spear shaft. It was good, solid oak. "You once enjoyed being spread with a branch to hold your legs apart. Do you still?"

In answer, Remo attacked one of Quenton's nipples, nibbling and biting on the firm flesh. One of his delicate hands reached down to cup Quenton's balls and massage them gently.

Quenton smiled and threw his head back, enjoying the dual sensations from a lover who knew precisely how to please. That Remo remembered as well as he did, even after so long, pleased Quenton. "I'll take that for a yes."

With a sly glance, Remo withdrew and danced away with a teasing grin. "I should make you catch me, as we often played."

"Too easy." Quenton lashed out with a bit of magic, catching Remo off guard and binding the Elf's ankles to the floor. "You forget you're not in the forest now, but upon man-made things."

Remo laughed, even as the magic moved, forcing him to spread his legs wide. "I forget nothing."

Quenton knelt before his Elf, spear shaft and straps in hand. He felt Remo grasp his hair, not only for balance but also for the pleasure of his dragon's lips wrapped around his cock. While Quenton's mouth watered, he had other plans. He tied one limb to the spear shaft where earlier he'd carved a notch to fit the

Elf's trim ankle, then repeated the procedure with the other ankle. Then, and only then, did Quenton's mouth and teeth find the inside of Remo's thigh. The Elf's cock twitched against his hair and cheek.

Remo groaned aloud. "Teasing dragon."

The dragon in question murmured against the tasty flesh, "I've barely begun to tease, lover. We have all night, since tomorrow is a rest day."

"Oh." Remo's hands were free to do what they wished, including fetch things with the simple Elven magic all the fair folk possessed. "Well then, perhaps you'll like what is in my hand." A small vial smacked into his palm.

Quenton eyed the odd bottle of dark red, viscous liquid. "What is that?"

Remo grinned. "A thing Prince Jack brought with him from the non-magic realm. It's called flavored lube. This one tastes like the finest berries, mixed with honey."

"Honey?" Quenton's greed for honey was the same as any other dragon. He all but snatched it from Remo's hands. "How do you use it?" There was no cork. "Better still, how do you get it open?"

Remo reached down to the odd white top and used his thumb to pop open a portion of the top. From a small hole rose a sweet, berry-laden scent. "Use a small amount anywhere you wish to lick or fuck." Suiting words to action, he tipped the bottle until a small drop fell onto the head of his cock, and he rubbed it in. "Taste."

Now that they were alone, Quenton could indulge his fondest wish and be himself in front of Remo. He flicked out his forked tongue and tickled both ends to do as commanded. The sweet liquid exploded with flavor on his tongue. "We must acquire this potion for ourselves. Perhaps someday the prince will take us to that mundane world?" He eagerly dribbled more on his lover's twitching flesh, allowing the liquid to flow gently down the valley of Remo's ass.

Remo moaned but wisely made no protests. His back arched, allowing Quenton's arms to lift and flip him on his stomach, making use of the soft quilted gambeson like a pillow. This game they'd played full often, and he would not interrupt while Quenton pretended to be the victor and he the helpless spoil of battle.

Quenton eyed with pleasure the tasty morsel quite literally spread before him. His tongue flickered to lick his lips, and his mouth watered to taste that moon-white flesh before the dessert of berry honey and rosy pink ass. His already heated cock hardened enough to pound dwarven metal. The sweet scent drove him nearly mad, but he disciplined himself not to bite but nibble.

The tasty muscle his teeth teased jumped and firmed while his Elf moaned and squirmed helplessly. "Teasing dragon!" was all he got out before Quenton's tongue found his ass and ate the berry honey from it with relish. Perhaps it was best Quenton's command of Elven was not extensive, judging by the colorful language spewing from his lover's pale lips.

"Tsk, tsk. Such a vocabulary. My noble ears burn. Perhaps you would prefer I did this?" Quenton lifted his face from between the two white globes of Remo's ass, squirted the liquid confidently back where he'd removed it, and stood to lift his Elf by the waist until Remo was impaled on his dragon's aching cock. Quenton turned, sat on the gambeson, and supported his Elf carefully between his legs like a delicate harp to be played. "Now you may bounce and ride to your heart's content."

Never one to be slow in reacting, Remo took quick advantage of the reversal and used his hands on Quenton's thighs to control his up and down motions despite the spear keeping his legs spread wide. "I could use magic or change back into a wyvern so I had wings to beat."

Quenton laughed. "And a tail to sting me? I think not, my lover Elf. I've just healed from the last buffeting. We will fly together without wings soon enough, for I fear my longing for you has made my body most anxious for release." He bit his own lip, praying for a few seconds more to give his love all the ecstasy desired by both.

Remo grunted with his own pleasure. "Indeed? Another time then, for I, too, am --" He interrupted his own sentence with a sharp, soft cry. His own orgasm flew skyward and glittered in the moonlight as it fell to the wooden floor.

Now Quenton felt safe in permitting himself release, and he let his own orgasm soar as if it had wings of its own. Soon he would be able to tell his Elf of his new quest, and they would celebrate Prince Jack's continued life.

They panted in each other's arms for a brief moment, and then Remo himself whisked away the spear spreader. "Sorry, my lover dragon, but that was growing uncomfortable."

Chuckling, Quenton fished his hand deep in his pack and brandished the distinctive blue bottle of Elven wine. "I knew you would when you were ready. I would keep you spread and available for my lust always, if I could."

The Elf mage snorted and manifested two goblets, floating midair and awaiting their fill of the sparkling liquid. "I know it, but we have better things to discuss than your fantasies. What did your queen say? Please tell me we will not be at odds."

Quenton filled the goblets and took one to salute his love with. "Indeed, we are not enemies, for my queen has given me a new task. I am now permitted -- nay, even ordered, though I would do it gladly in any case -- to befriend Prince Jack and ascertain if he is indeed as noble and true as you say."

Remo sipped delicately from his goblet and raised one silver eyebrow at his dragon. "Indeed? That is good news on the surface, but would it not be easier simply to be honest with the prince?"

"That's what I'd prefer."

Both Quenton and Remo started guiltily and spun around. Leaning against the door was Jack himself, with Aneurin hovering disapprovingly in the background of the starry night.

Jack pushed himself casually away from the doorframe and sauntered in. "Gentlemen, in the language of my adopted world, you have some explaining to do."

Chapter Four

Duplicity. Plainly, Remo would be accused of the dishonorable crime. He hung his head, knowing such a charge could easily be laid upon him with no small amount of truth.

Quenton stammered and choked on his wine, at a complete loss.

Jack ushered his dragon inside, then closed the door firmly. His face was grim, but not angry. "You guys really don't know much about humans, do you?" He shook his head and sat on a bench.

"They know even less about you." Aneurin quietly gave Quenton one sniff, raised his eyebrows, and sat down on another bench near the door.

Many might assume Jack's bond mate guarded their meeting, but Remo wasn't fooled. He was far enough away not to crush Jack if he changed and charred the miscreants to ash before Quenton could also shift.

Quenton gave Aneurin's position a nod of acknowledgement. "I remind you I breathe poisonous breath that harms the skin as well. Let's not think of killing our loves before we have given full consideration of all."

"Remind me to discuss that with you, if your breath is chlorine, as the myth… legends tell."

Jack cleared his throat and held up a conciliatory hand. "Ease up, guys. No one needs to get mad. I think we need to have a -- truth-telling -- session."

Quenton nodded. "This I agree to do. But why do you stumble over your words so?"

Remo answered for Jack, whose lips were twitching with suppressed laughter. "I remind you that Jack is from the non-magic realm. His language was different, and I think we would not recognize his phrasing were he to directly translate. Some words require a cultural reference."

Aneurin's mutter from the door was nonetheless audible to all. "You don't know the half of it."

Jack manifested a steaming mug in his hands, causing Remo to start. "Sorry. Finally caught the hang of teleporting objects tonight, and I see no reason to waste a perfectly good cup of ja... coffee." He grinned. "See? There's an example. I almost called this brew in my hands by one of its many nicknames, java, named for one of the places where the ingredients come from."

Quenton sipped his wine, feigning more aplomb than he possessed. Remo could feel the twang of his nervousness like badly tuned harp strings. "This explains much. We did wonder whence you came, and how you got to the human realm."

Remo caught Aneurin's wince and wondered at such an emotional reaction to a simple statement. "This sounds like a tale."

Jack's frown deepened, and he sipped his hot beverage, his eyes clouded with thought. "A long one we don't have time for. What the non-human allies seek to know probably boils down to a few sentences. The rest can wait." He took another sip. "You can ask Aneurin for details later, okay? He's better at this than I am."

"Then tell your allies what they need to know, Prince Jack." Quenton leaned forward eagerly.

"My father tried to steal me on the night of my birth, probably to be a blood sacrifice." Jack paused and his words faltered, stopping and starting as if he chose his words with great care. "He failed, but he created his own enemy that night. Bad enough when you're evil to those who have a chance to walk away, but babies? Kids? Mother hid me away where I'd be very difficult to find, but she couldn't erase all those first five years of living in Honalee. I grew up with a fascination for creatures that didn't exist in that mundane realm." The loving smile he bestowed on Aneurin could have lit the entire room.

Aneurin's golden eyes were the lamps that reflected the light of that love.

"Jack and I bonded early, but were forced to separate often. We have not had more than a few months together as adults to fly as we ought. That's why we're so clumsy."

"Yeah well, what's done can't be undone." Jack stood up and paced around the salle, never getting out of earshot. "I just hope that sonovabitch who fathered me didn't sacrifice my little sister. I'd like to have a sister, and not just because she'd be the heir to the throne."

Remo bit his lip, hard. The growl had ended on such a wistful note, but now was not the time to reveal all. Instead, he too would reserve his grander tales for another day. "I believe it is now my turn, for it is a short story. In the past few centuries, it has been deemed unwise to bond with a dragon. The last Elf who did died at the breath of his own dragon. He was my uncle, and my first teacher."

Quenton reached out and caressed Remo's trembling hand. "To love a dragon is…" He grimaced. "The Elves say it is the same as loving a beast."

Jack's grimace matched his own. "Gotcha. Say no more." Jack met Aneurin's loving gaze. "But you, Quenton, have the most explaining to do of all. I think I've been remarkably patient in waiting to find out why a dragon pretends to be a human lord and then is ordered by his queen to befriend me."

Remo could not spare his love this task. It was Quenton's burden and duty, and Remo would surely lay bare all instead of what was necessary. All he could do instead was lay his head upon Quenton's shoulder and offer his unspoken support, so he did.

Quenton caressed his hair with his cheek and sighed. "Indeed, you have been most patient, Prince Jack." He drew one deep breath, and plunged as if he dove off a cliff. "I have been a spy in your father's court since Cadell usurped the throne. His hatred of dragon kind is well known."

Jack's lips twitched. "Go on, Quenton. I can see how having you there would be useful, and with good reason, I'm sure."

"That also explains the bathing in garlic." Aneurin's nose wrinkled. "Those of us who are bonded are less trusted by the independent dragons. Who knew if one of us would foolishly betray Quenton if we sniffed out what he was?"

Quenton jerked a short nod of his chin. "I'll be grateful to smell like a dragon again, 'tis true. May I never smell the stench of garlic again once I am free." He stared defiantly at Prince Jack. "A few weeks ago, my task changed. The Dragon's Stone was stolen from our queen's lair."

Remo raised his hand. "Permit me to remove the frown from Jack's face. The Dragon's Stone is an ancient artifact created by a wizard who loved dragons, but could not bond with one. No dragon would have him, and so his obsession grew into madness. He created the stone and infused it with all his mage energy and his wish to control dragon kind." He gave a wry smile for the irony of it all. "In his madness, he fed all into it, including his own life force. But, in doing so, the madness was purged from him though we knew it not. His young daughter found his body and the stone. She was the first to bond with it."

Now Quenton resumed the tale. "She was an honorable woman and a good sorceress. She recognized the stone's power, and though she could not free herself of it, she united the humans and forced peace upon Honalee for the first time. She was the first queen of Honalee. Upon her death she saw to it the stone was returned to us so others less scrupulous would have no chance to control dragon kind."

A long, low whistle expressed Jack's understanding. "Yeah, I can see why you dragons would want that rock back, especially if Cadell stole it. Such a thing would be right up his alley."

"So what does this have to do with befriending Jack?" Aneurin put in. "We've tried to make it very clear that Jack doesn't want to be associated with his father, and even actively opposes him."

Remo nodded and raised his head from Quenton's warm shoulder. Now he must dance delicately toward a truth Jack would not like. "This is known, though it is always good to hear such statements often. Remember that the stone has the spirit of the once-mad wizard within it? The wizard still loves the dragon race, and will in times of crisis seek one of his own kind, hoping that a human will prove to be an honorable hero to protect and love dragons as he does."

Jack's eyes narrowed slightly, and his face became blank and lax. "Cadell only thinks he has the stone. It's bonded with a human, hasn't it?"

Quenton sighed. "Aye. It has."

Aneurin sat still as stone. His eyes flickered once to his bonded, and then studied the floor as if he would find the answers in the sanded wood beneath his feet.

"Shit." Jack's face fell, and he resumed his agitated pacing. "Great. Just fucking great. Why can't I be an ordinary dragon-riding, gay wizard instead of an heir to the throne foretold hero? You guys act like I'm some sort of messiah. Glorious destinies usually end with glorious funerals. I don't walk on water or do funny things with loaves and fishes, either."

Remo burst out laughing. "You've been listening to too many bards, Prince Jack. I don't know what a messiah is, but since you fear it so, I think we can safely assume you will not be one. They may not exist here."

Jack ground his teeth, then chuckled. "I'll remember to keep my mouth shut." He sent his coffee cup away with a flourish. "Okay then. If the damned stone has bonded to me, then you need me for something."

Aneurin stood away from his post and marched to stand shoulder-to-shoulder with his bonded love.

"What a magnificent pair they are," Remo mused. Like shadows of dark and darker still, with pale wraith-like skin, one with eyes of translucent gold and the other pair deep forest moss. Not like the legends of golden-haired princes fighting off terrible evils, but mortal and accessible.

Quenton grinned and strode forward to clasp Jack on the shoulder. "Your task is the easiest and the hardest, my friend." He paused and swept his arm to encompass the night out the windows. "Point the way."

Both Jack and Aneurin looked about in confusion.

Coaxingly, Remo whispered, "You are the lodestone, Jack. Only you can point to the Dragon's Stone unerringly, no matter how far away."

Quenton looked at them both in exasperation. "Lift your hand and point, Jack."

"Back off." Jack's growl surprised them all. "I'm under enough pressure here." When no one moved, he raised an eyebrow. "Back away, please."

Remo wondered at the light of mischief in his eyes, but obeyed, dragging the stunned Quenton with him.

"You too, lover dragon. Do me a favor and guard the door. I'm going to feel pretty silly if this fails." Jack patted Aneurin's cheek and gave him one quick kiss. "We may need saddles."

"I think not, Prince Jack. The Stone has manifested here. It would be reluctant to leave you." Quenton leaned casually against the wall and folded his arms.

"The stone had no choice! I was forced to give it to Tilda after the trial." Sighing, Jack stepped to the center of the room, lifted his arm, shut his eyes, and spun like a child's toy. He hummed a few bars from a nonsense child's verse, "Ring around the Rosie."

His song surprised even Jack himself, and yet it fit in a weird way to be singing a medieval song about the symptoms of the Black Plague. For when he finished the verse, his finger pointed up and away to the mountains above the school.

Jack opened his eyes and looked grimly outside the window. "Figures. Up into the mountains, where legend has it dragons cannot survive the cold. I know a few species of dragon can indeed survive up there, but I'm not sure cold drakes and ice dragons would be cooperative right now. Anyone got a spare yeti?"

"Huh?" they all chorused.

"Never mind. Flying is still faster than climbing before the dragons go into torpor. I'll teleport a few supplies in. Come on, Aneurin. Leave them alone for a few." Jack strode purposely for the door and wrenched it open.

Obediently, Aneurin followed his love out. "Why?"

Jack's eyes twinkled with mischief. "I figure Remo will not waste this opportunity to fly, and I think wyverns are cold-hardy to a certain point. Since we need Quenton hale and hearty, he can't piss Remo off." He waved a dismissive hand in Quenton's direction. "Situation is reversed, old boy. Start sucking."

* * *

The massive wooden doors creaked like an old woman's bones and twice as loud. No light flared up, no sleepy stableman's voice called out asking who was there.

Quenton whooshed out a breath in relief. One final obstacle before they flew into the mountains, and for him, the most terrifying. He eyed Prince Jack with envy, for Jack at least had both parents he could say he knew well enough to like or dislike. Quenton could not say that, and wondered if perhaps he was better off not knowing. His booted feet crunched softly in the hay littering the floor. Before he and Aneurin changed form for flight, they needed certain things to be found only here.

Aneurin's voice filtered as soft as a breeze into his mind. "Jack wants to know if you're sure this is where they keep the fur-lined cloaks as well as the saddles. He found the saddles and has teleported mine and one that should fit you outside."

Remo's butt wiggled right next to Jack's as they rummaged in a deep trunk. His Elf's decision to ride on his back instead of flying at his side both relieved and disappointed Quenton. Relieved, because wyverns were so irascible and noisy. Disappointed because he so desperately wanted to be free in the skies with his little love.

Silently, two glowing silver eyes rose above the wall next to the storage shed where Jack and Remo moved to the next trunk, oblivious to the danger. Only those shining ovals showed in the faint lamplight, but Quenton swallowed, knowing who they belonged to -- Watash, the dragon bonded to that crazy wizard DeAngelo, who taught dragon riding lessons at the school.

Gathering up his courage, Quenton tried bravado. "Gentle folk…"

"*Shhh*!"

A loud hiss followed. "Is this some foolish student prank?" Watash was definitely not amused. "Tell me I do not need to call DeAngelo from his slumbers to discipline you four miscreants." He sniffed the air. "Oh. Hello, son. You need a bath."

Quenton jumped back several feet and landed in a pile of hay. Shock drained his face of blood, and he lay where he was, unable to maintain any pretense of dignity. "You… you know who I am?"

Jack, Remo, and Aneurin all crowded outside the shed door, looking sheepish. Jack muttered in a strange voice, "Cheese it, boys. It's the cops. The jig is up."

Watash gave Jack one snort of laughter and turned back to Quenton. "Of course I do. Hang on. Let me put my book down. Then you boys can explain to me why you're skulking around stealing saddles long after dark." His head disappeared, and a loud *thunk* signaled the book's closure.

Remo glided over in that peculiar Elven silent stalk and gave Quenton a hand up so he stood on his own two feet. "Told you a bath would be wise." He stood shoulder to shoulder with Quenton. "I thought dragons didn't care about who sired them?"

Quenton licked his lips. "I care." Oh, yes, more than he wanted to admit.

"As do I." Watash walked around the corner of his stall and into the open area outside the storage sheds. His iron gray hair was as full as a lion's mane and his overall appearance matched, save he wore dark blue clothes. A powerful old lion, still full able to rend and tear, but preferring a place in the sun to rest. "Maybe I've lived too long among humans. Now out with it. I shall not ask again."

Jack stepped forward. "We think we know where the Stone is, Watash." His arm pointed unerringly toward the mountains to the east. "Up there."

Watash rubbed his chin and smiled when Aneurin stepped protectively beside Jack. "No need, Aneurin. No need at all. So you did bond with it, did you? Sounds like we need a bit of a skull session. Come to my stall. Who wants coffee, tea, or beer?"

While they all acquired their choice of beverage from the stove or chill chest, Watash made himself comfortable in one of the many chairs available. "I spend most of the year here, so bigawd I'm comfortable with good lamps and furniture for guests. Too bad I can't have a proper nest, though. Coins are singularly inadequate without a few gems to make it pretty." He waved expansively at his coppery bed of coins.

Jack sipped from his choice of a huge fired clay mug filled with coffee. He gave a sigh of contentment and took a chair near Watash. "Okay, pal. You sounded completely unsurprised that I've bonded with the Stone. Why?"

Aneurin saluted Watash with his mug of tea. "I can answer that in part. The teachers have suspected it since the Trial, Jack. DeAngelo would have been informed of the possibility, and told to watch Watash for signs of control." He paused and waited for Watash's nod. "Not to mention the way all dragon kind seems to flock to our company despite our being the worst students."

Watash shrugged. "That's the long and short of it. DeAngelo has been spending a lot of time being ingratiating to that…" He drew in a deep breath and visibly calmed himself. "The headmistress. I don't have to tell you to be careful, do I, son? Something's not quite right about this."

"Yes, sire. I agree, but I cannot put a fang into this meat." Quenton paced. "In all my years in the royal palace, I have seen no despotism, no blood rites, only quiet management and an air of waiting. What was he waiting for?" Quenton studied Prince Jack. "You?"

Remo folded his arms. "The usurper may have made a serious mistake if he thinks he can corrupt Prince Jack."

"Thanks, I think," Jack muttered and got up to pace. "I've been poor and I've been rich. Rich is better, but I've got that anytime I want. Love?" He grinned at Aneurin. "Got that, too."

Watash took a healthy slug from a bottle of beer and burped yeastily. "Damn me if I can puzzle it out what bait he'll use on you. Money, sex, and power cover the basic greed of all humankind, and you have all three in your grasp already. The next step would be to threaten Aneurin in some way, but this would be foolish on his part. Unless he can get Aneurin badly injured -- difficult at best -- then it's unlikely." He huffed out a breath of smoke. "Add to this you can summon all dragon kind into that cave, and I hope he's aware we'll remove the remains with a sponge. I'd love to go with you, but I'm a bit slower in my old age. Besides, you know DeAngelo. He'd take over, and I can't just walk out on my own bond mate."

Remo's eyes narrowed at Watash, but he shrugged. "Understandable, Watash. Don't trouble yourself. Just tell us where the fur-lined cloaks are stored, and we'll let you get some sleep."

"Last shed on the north wall. You'll also find some good lanterns, some rope, dried foodstuffs, water skins, weapons, and a well-stocked herbal pack. Occasionally, DeAngelo takes a recalcitrant student group on a live-training adventure. They usually come back with their attitudes much more inclined to obey orders."

Aneurin and Remo took themselves off in the direction of the shed. Watash followed Jack and Quenton out to where the saddles lay on convenient benches where the wet dew would not make them uncomfortable. He even helped Jack adjust the school saddle until it fitted Quenton's dragon form about as well as could be expected, then helped them distribute supplies and weapons.

Jack patted the last strap into place on Aneurin's purple body and saluted Watash with a cheeky grin. "If we don't return in two days, send out the posse, will you?"

Remo clambered up on his dragon saddle for the first time, grunting with the effort and tangling himself in his bow until he settled. "What would we need a cat for?"

Watash chuckled, but Jack remained stone-faced, even grim. "Posse is a type of rescue party, my friend. Let's get airborne. We're wasting the cover of darkness with all this chit-chat."

Aneurin and Quenton jumped into the wind simultaneously, snapping wings open with a disregard for the shower of dirt and pebbles below as they struggled to get aloft in the thick, cold night air.

The icy wind made thinking difficult, and Quenton had not flown much in the past twenty years. He'd pay for this night with sore muscles. Quenton waited until they were out of range of easy communication, and whispered in Remo's mind. "Are you as suspicious as I am of what just happened?"

The Elf mage growled back into his mind, "If you're only suspicious, then I'm a brownie. You're smarter than that. Watash was coerced. Want to bet they have the old wizard? The only way to threaten a dragon is to harm his weaker bondmate. Watash was aching to go with us, and was hoping we'd ask our dragon instructor to accompany us. Tell Aneurin, so he can tell Jack."

Quenton nodded, and his eyes unfocused as he passed on the message.

"We've got to go back and rescue DeAngelo!" Jack raged in his saddle and tugged futilely on his saddle handle.

"Wait, listen to the rest, Jack." Aneurin wisely ignored the agitated yanks on his saddle and flew for the cavern now locked in dawn's shadow.

Quenton relayed all this back to Remo and fervently wished for willow bark tea. He was getting a headache, and his flight muscles stabbed like knives in his chest. When this was all over, he intended to get back in flight form if it killed him.

Remo, bless him, put the rest succinctly. "Jack, the wizard DeAngelo would be out of his dragon's reach. They'd take him to the caverns where the cold would kill an older dragon like Watash."

Jack released his saddle and snarled at the ever-approaching dark maw of a large cavern entrance that whistled with the icy dawn wind. "I don't get it. Why do anything to the old guy? He's loonier than a goony, but harmless. And why tell Watash to encourage us to go?"

Even Aneurin's voice shivered, now. "Because they want us up here for some reason, and DeAngelo was going to stop us or warn us. Remember what Watash said? DeAngelo had been sucking up to the headmistress? Watash was displeased with the headmistress. I'll bet she's the primary kidnapper. She's made it clear she's very loyal to Cadell."

Quenton nodded, surprised at this weaving of known facts, but he was much more anxious to put his claws down on that solid ledge and furl his aching wings. He groaned as he did so, and stepped politely aside so Aneurin could land. "Excellent deductions, Aneurin, and worthy of a dragon spy. I'll nominate you to replace me at court, since you'll be there anyway when Jack is crowned."

"Crowned my ass." Jack jumped down to Aneurin's foreleg and thence to the ground, as effortlessly as a dragonrider of legend. "I don't want to be king. Come on, scaly butts. Transform so we can get you into these fur-lined cloaks."

Aneurin transformed quickly and practically fell into the cloak his mate held for him. "There is something to be said for being a mammal, and I mean besides a hairless ape's opposable thumb."

Shivering enough to make his bones rattle, Quenton managed a change with difficulty, but Remo was there waiting with his cloak. All Quenton could do was keep his teeth from breaking with the force of the chattering they did. "Shouldn't we be quiet?"

His darling Elf wrapped him tighter in the cloak and fed him a sip of warm tea from a small skin. All he could see of him were those grass green eyes and the tip of his nose in his own furs, but he could hear the amusement in his voice. "Why bother? They know we're coming."

A light flared from deep within the cavern, arresting their attention.

Jack sighed and tucked his wand up his sleeve. "Yep, they sure do, and we're already in deep shit."

Chapter Five

Remo opened his mouth, intent upon easing the prince's fears and adding a word or two of caution to see what game the usurper played. The light gave warning that they were not only expected, but also awaited. Somehow Remo doubted they'd be served tea and canapés.

Jack edged away from the light, and his half-smile was calculating. "Assume the worst and hope for the best, gentle folk." He assumed a pleasant demeanor, but the crafty smile remained for an instant more. "Remember, since Cadell knows we're coming, there's no sense in hiding. He could have destroyed us at any time. After all, he's the king. Therefore, he wants something. Our duty is to find out what it is he wants."

Aneurin studied the rocks above the cavern, but he nodded at each salient point. The gray stone rock and maw of the cavern did not look interesting in the slightest. If anything, the foreboding darkness cloaked everything in a depressing fog of sameness.

Never let it be said Remo's dragon love was slow to understand a warning. Quenton's half-smile was as intelligent and full of guile as Jack's, and they appeared as alike as brothers despite their myriad differences. Black and moss eyes glittered like dew in the morning, then went as innocent and sweet as a young fawn. Remo shivered to see the duplicity possible when humans and dragons decided the cause was worth skirting the edge of dishonor's sharp blade. Humans could be so blithe about deception it amazed Remo still. Yet by his silence Remo gave consent, so he agreed once more to share the duplicity.

Jack gave Remo a somewhat weary smile and took the lead. He stepped into the cavern and directly into the path of the light seemingly without fear.

Aneurin lingered, gesturing courteously to urge Remo forward, and Remo then understood the game. The purpose was to learn what Cadell wanted and to let him think that they were fools who went willingly into the trap. Remo, with his youthful face and small stature, appeared no older than the human prince. That appearance had caused Remo much hardship upon occasion, but here it had a use. Also, Cadell hated dragons. By the dragons showing Jack and Remo honor, Cadell would assume them "tamed" and therefore docile. Perhaps that would be his biggest error, if he did not underestimate his son.

A long, well-hewn hall led them deep underground, though the height of the ceiling above was too great for dwarf mines. The sides and top of the hall were shored up like a mine, giving Remo great puzzlement. Who else but a dwarf or gnome would live and mine in this cold, forbidden climate? Then Remo saw the reason. The wall glittered with a tiny vein of platinum, too small to be worth digging out, even for a dragon.

His heart sank, and Remo noted that poor Quenton's hand trembled as he too recognized the metal so essential to dragon breath. The humans mined out the rare platinum to deny young dragons the ability to use their breath weapons. Especially for the largest group of dragons, the fire-breathers, platinum provided the essential first spark that lit the air from a dragon's body. Even those who breathed other deadly substances needed the impetus of a small fire spark to provide the explosive force to push the air far enough away from a dragon's sensitive eyes.

Without fanfare, the cavern opened up into a great room, large enough to house several dragons and their riders without anyone feeling crowded. This would have been the room where the ore was sorted, for humans wasted nothing. At the far end, near a fireplace so large several humans could stand upright within, sat Cadell the Usurper. Ostentatiously, he even wore the royal crown of state, despite it being too small to fit well upon his head. It perched there, ludicrously small, like a bright hummingbird upon a gray boulder.

Cadell nodded his iron gray head, as if counting them off to make sure the whole of his guest list had arrived. He gestured to the six chairs arranged around his throne-like seat, offering them their choice. "Sit, sit, boys. I'm sure you have a thousand questions. Wine?"

A huge tray appeared, full of wines of every description and glasses to match every need. It hovered for a moment, and then settled upon a knee table placed precisely in the center of the conversation grouping.

Jack shrugged and sniffed bottles until he found something he liked. "Thanks, Dad. I figure you won't bother to poison us. You could have done that at any time at school." He poured some beverage that was honey brown and saluted the man in the throne with irreverent cheek.

"Oh, so you acknowledge the relationship? Good. I do not wish to waste time explaining who I am." The king was perfectly at ease, and poured himself a wine the color of blueberries.

"Yeah, I know who you are. How's the leg?" Jack sipped delicately, and poured Remo a glass of fine Elven fruit wine. "Here you go, Remo. Great stuff. Dad's not skimping on the hospitality."

Remo winced, for Jack had to know the king had a wooden leg and it was said he was sensitive about mentioning his deformity.

The king twitched his robes aside, revealing one hairy human shank, and an intricately carved wooden leg. "Well enough, and you're insolent."

Jack shrugged. "Hey, sorry for not falling in with your plans to be a blood sacrifice before I was a few hours old, pal. Not my idea of a good time."

Quenton remained standing, coming to rest his arms at the top of his chair. His demeanor was that of a relaxed and lazy human noble, but his agitation vibrated along their bond like a plucked harp string, discordant and uncomfortable. Unnerved by the mining of essential platinum and feeling more than a bit trapped, both of them fed on each other's fears and worries until Remo grew concerned that they would broadcast their distress to anyone with the ability to hear.

Cadell threw back his head and laughed heartily. "Is that what you've been told all these years as to why I tried to steal you? Well, no wonder!" He put up one hand, palm out, for a brief moment. "I admit to dabbling in blood magic, but I wouldn't kill another intelligent being. Goes against the grain, thanks. No son, I stole you to save you."

Jack's eyes widened, and Aneurin, who had been lingering in the outer circle, stepped forward a pace. Remo gave credit to Jack for aplomb. He recovered quickly, and sipped his wine. "Save me from what?"

"Why, if you haven't figured it out by now, I shall be disappointed in your intelligence." Cadell's right hand slapped the arm of his throne. "Damn it all, Jack, do you really wish to be a second-class citizen and stud stallion to a pile of spoiled sorceresses?"

This was not how Remo expected the conversation to go, and judging by the looks on his companions' faces all were startled by this turn of events. Aneurin looked positively white, with the firelight creating an almost skeletal appearance to his thin features. A mirror above the mantle reflected Quenton's face of stone, not even his eyes glittered as he held his secrets close to his heart and mind.

Jack, however, did not bother to hide his astonishment. His jaw dropped, and his eyes grew wide. Remo did not recognize the language pouring from his lips, but the rasping tone conveyed his angry thoughts well enough. Then he seemed to gather his thoughts and spoke Honalean. "You have my attention now. Tell me, what was your scheme? Raising a newborn infant would not have been easy."

Cadell settled back in his throne. "I wouldn't have been alone." Lady Tilda appeared from behind a tapestry, showing another mineshaft before the heavy drapery flipped back into place. "Tilda was quite willing to help me, weren't you, my dear?"

"Of course, darling." Tilda walked silently and gracefully to kneel on a cushion beside Cadell's throne, and her smile was not pleasant. Today she wore a blue gown that matched her eyes, though one could not have called it modest. It was slit up both sides to show off long, excellent legs, and the deep plunge showed off far more of her spectacular figure than it covered. Most interestingly, around her neck was a leather band similar to what humans put around their hunting hounds, even down to the small silver loop in front for a leash. Most intriguing.

Jack took in her appearance, and one side of his lips quirked for an instant. "Forgive me if I'm glad you didn't have to resort to such measures. While my childhood wasn't perfect, it did have moments of glory." His smile at Aneurin was full of love and perhaps full of hidden tales.

Aneurin stepped from the shadows beyond the circle of chairs to take his hand. "Yes, it turned out well enough."

Oh, yes, there definitely was a story to be told. That much was now clear. Jack's eyes were haunted, and Remo wondered what horrors a child could face in the mundane world. Still, he resolved to hold his peace.

Quenton shifted behind his chair and sent a warning of his role down their bond. He stepped to the side of his chair and arrogantly planted his buttocks on the arm of another. "Yes, yes, don't get sloppy, Prince Jack. Can't you see the king is not finished telling you his view of events past? I for one am most anxious to hear this. Please continue, Your Majesty." Quenton leaned forward, seemingly avid to hear more, though Remo heard his one true burning question -- where was the Stone?

Cadell favored Quenton with a narrow-eyed glance, but accepted his love's attention as his due. Could it be possible the King of humans had not discovered Quenton was a dragon in disguise? "Thank you, Lord Quenton. My scheme, as you put it, Mikalus -- my apologies, I understand you prefer to be called Jack -- was simple, if long in the execution. My whole purpose has been to prove by any means necessary that men are worthy to be equal to women, despite some obvious differences. To that end, I intended to raise you in my home where I ruled, not a woman. I did not care if you were to be a male or female, though a female would have suited me better, I admit. I did not plan to lose my leg that night, nor that your mother would secret you in the mundane realm to hide you after my next attempt failed."

At that moment, Remo was struck with the similarity between Jack and Cadell. While Cadell's hair had turned to iron gray, it fell in the same soft waves as Jack's dark brown. Moss green and brown eyes shot with gold stared back and forth like a mirror image, one young and strong, one old and bent with age. Both were still incredibly handsome despite Jack's starveling appearance.

Lady Tilda sniffed. "What fool sends a five-year-old wizard with a dragon nursemaid who doesn't speak the language or understand the culture into another world so ill-prepared? Your mother deserved to lose you."

Jack's hands fisted at his side. His jaw was clenched so tightly, Remo wondered he didn't hear Jack's teeth shatter. He took a deep breath and ground out a request. "I would prefer if you did not slander my mother, Lady Tilda."

Lady Tilda settled back on her cushion and thrust out her chin defiantly.

Aneurin shook, on the verge of pure rage. "Same here. My mother did the best she could with what she had."

At Aneurin's growl, Lady Tilda seemed to shrink in on herself, cowed at last.

Remo had to speak, hoping to glean more tidbits from the Usurper. "So, you wanted to steal your son or daughter to raise them in an unreal state of equality? To what end? The noblewomen were not likely to decide upon the word of two wizards that all humans should be equal."

"I think he hoped the oppressed male nobles and other wizards would join him in expressing the wish for a more egalitarian society. I cannot say I was looking forward to stud service as if I had no preferences of my own." Quenton shrugged. "I do like to sport, but that is not all that I am."

Remo swallowed a snicker at the double entendre, for he knew Quenton was his, heart and soul. No female of any race had ever caught Quenton's eye despite their many blandishments. Those dark eyes were for Remo alone and had been for well over a hundred years. Not that he'd counted.

Now it was Cadell's turn to snort. "Nor any man, I think. While we do enjoy our pleasures, we do think with more than our cocks. Well, I considered myself a fortunate man when I discovered the world your mother had deposited you into. Lo and behold, a place where men and women were nearly equal, with some allowances made for strength or individuality. I could have sung for joy." The king sat back in his chair with a pleased smile upon his face.

"We elected to leave you in that dreary place, Jack." Tilda settled herself upon her cushion and took Cadell's hand. "By that point of course, Princess Miranda was under Cadell's care, and -- forgive me -- she served our purposes better. You were there in case we needed you, safe and sound."

Jack toyed with his wineglass without drinking, his eyes dark and moody. "Not exactly, but I can see you'd think so." He put his wineglass down with a sharp crack on the knee table that sat between them. "So, your scheme was to raise up at least one or more examples of wizards and sorceresses who understood the idea of males being equal to females? Did you intend to put my sister on the throne as a puppet ruler with you calling the shots behind the curtain, telling her how to change the laws?"

Remo saw easily how the plan could have worked. With Princess Miranda thoroughly indoctrinated in the concept of equality for both genders, she would have been appalled at the way males were treated. She would have been happy to change the laws. Worse, if she had failed to materialize, Jack would have served despite his masculinity and inability to produce a female heir. Such things had happened before. No doubt a substitute could be found to father an heir.

Cadell pounded his hand down on the arm of his throne. "Yes, damn them all! How could so many innocent fools thwart me? Your mother and her dragon, and then all my careful plans unraveled before my eyes when Miranda disappeared with her nurse!" He whipped out a wand and entangled Remo in a web spell before Remo could stop him. "Where did you Elves take her?" What had Jack said earlier? The jig was up.

* * *

A creak of wood sliding against wood rasped so quietly Quenton almost missed the sound. Quenton froze, afraid to even duck or indicate in any way that he had noted that ominous telltale of an arrow about to be fired. But at whom was the arrow targeted?

Remo's eyes widened slightly. He too had heard the rasp in the stunned silence that followed Cadell's demand. He could barely breathe with the lash of power pinning his body to the chair, but he managed a calm answer. "I don't know where she is, though I have my suspicions. Would you care to hear them?"

Quenton swallowed. Remo played a dangerous game to bait the madman, but now that his love had pointed out the obvious, Quenton, too, joined in. "What would you do with the princess if she were to appear, Usurper?"

Jack snorted. Quenton pitied him for a moment, since his human ears could not detect the arrow's warning rasp. "Kind of obvious, isn't it? He'd hope to still rule through my little sister. I think you'd have a shock coming, Pops."

Aneurin glanced over at Quenton. His ears were sensitive enough, and he had the alarmed look of one who feared the worst. He took on the stiff look of one who girded himself for battle, and drew deep breaths. Quenton was grateful for the fire-breather, for his poisonous breath could not be easily controlled; however, dragon fire might be the very thing.

Cadell kept the charming aplomb that so marked him and his son, managing to remain handsome even while furious and confident of victory. "Of course I intend to suggest to Miranda what laws to repeal and replace. If she has been raised by barbaric Elves in a forest, she'll have not one whit of knowledge on how to rule wisely and well. She'll need a firm hand."

Lady Tilda's hand crept downward toward the base of the cushion where she knelt. Her skimpy costume did not allow for a place to hide a wand, but no doubt she'd stowed it beneath the cushion.

Quenton dared not move. He prayed with all his heart that the archer behind him was friend, not Royal Guard. There was no way to know with certainty. If Quenton used his breath, he'd kill friend as well as foe. If he changed to dragon, he still could not break his magical bonds unless he killed the Usurper and somehow managed to deal with Lady Tilda as well. One move toward his wand in his wrist sheath, and either the archer, Cadell, or Tilda would have him bound as well. Quenton trembled with the need to do something -- anything!

The twang of an arrow signaled the archer had made his or her decision. The arrow sang by his head and buried itself through Lady Tilda's arm and into the wooden leg of the throne.

Tilda screeched in pain, distracting Cadell for that critical instant that makes all the difference in battles won or lost.

Both Aneurin and Quenton took the opportunity to dive to the floor and come up as their natural selves, dragons ready to rend, with magic-resistant scales and bonded loves to defend.

Jack snatched the wand from Cadell's hand and snapped it across his knee. He wasted no time worrying about what happened to the pieces, but struck, one half of the wand still in his hand, his fist burying itself in Cadell's soft stomach.

Cadell fell back into his throne, jarring it. Tilda screamed once and fainted.

Remo flexed his full Elf-mage strength and broke his bonds with the same snapping sound as the wand's shattering. He shot out of his chair, both hands full of power, not bothering with a clumsy human wand. Now his will controlled a power such as the human could not understand, and the wood of Cadell's chair sprouted new branches that grew to bind the usurper in place. One branch grew over his mouth and acted like a horse's bridle, permitting him air, but not speech.

The fight had taken less than thirty heartbeats.

Quenton's pride in his Elf swelled further at Remo's calm demeanor. Moments before, Remo had been captured and threatened. Now he appeared calmly ready for a stroll in the woods.

Remo raised his head with a smile. "You've learned your lessons well, my daughter. Come forth and meet your brother and allies."

"Daughter?" Jack's jaw fell open. "Um, I thought you… er, that is…" He looked at Quenton, confused, as if to ask, "But I thought he loved you?"

"Adopted daughter." Princess Miranda stepped out from behind a pillar, her gray mottled tunic and trews and dirty face in no way hiding the moss green and gold eyes that were Cadell's heritage, though her short hair was the bright gold of her mother's. Even if Quenton were not inclined to such things, he could not help but notice Miranda had a most spectacular figure. Her bow was easily as large as most male Elves carried, and the muscles of her arms verified she could pull it.

Aneurin returned to human form. "So you were the sound I heard in the rocks earlier." He smiled and bowed. "Welcome home, Princess."

Jack snickered but held up a conciliatory hand when Miranda frowned at him. "Forgive me. The thought has occurred to me that you don't look like you're going to let Cadell influence anyone, much less you."

Miranda turned a steely glance upon Cadell and snorted. "Not likely, or I'll have him gagged. Your regency ended several years ago, Father. It just didn't suit me to come back. I was happy living with the Elves, and I wouldn't call any race barbaric when they have a written historical library that spans many thousands of years."

Cadell recoiled at her sneer, but his speech remained unintelligible. His fingers drummed on his throne in a staccato beat.

Quenton took pity on the pinned and unconscious Lady Tilda, still bleeding at Cadell's feet. He changed form, edged around the tableau, and wrenched the arrow from the chair, but did not risk removing it from her arm, where a broken bone grated audibly. Quenton doubted she'd wave a wand with that hand ever again, but she would not bleed to death. No matter what her crimes, she did not deserve to die.

Aneurin moved to help him. They bound her arm with the two pieces of Cadell's wand and a bit of the hem of her outlandish costume.

Remo nodded once and smiled at Quenton for aiding Tilda. He then put his arm protectively around the tall Miranda's waist. "I adopted Miranda when it became clear she would have sorceress powers as well as all the skills we Elves could impart to a short-lived human. She has been a full adult among us for only a few years, but enough to finish maturing."

"You make her sound like a bottle of wine, Remo." Jack grinned at Miranda. "I'm not too clear on how protocol goes, but it seems to me that one thing needs to happen." He turned around and removed the crown from Cadell's head, ignoring Cadell's furious glance. "Here, sister of mine. Crown yourself, because I don't think there's anyone here qualified." He then knelt and handed the crown to Miranda.

Miranda sighed. "You don't want it, either?"

Jack chuckled. "No. And you're the girl. Female. Woman. Whatever. You're the heir, not me."

Miranda muttered under her breath, "There goes my freedom." She placed the crown on her own tangled short hair. "I probably look ludicrous with a dirty face and scout wear. Stars, this means I have to wear a dress." Her disgusted tone made her feelings obvious.

Jack roared with laughter. "Don't fuss. I have to wear one too, and don't tell me wizard's robes aren't dresses."

He sobered. "I have a feeling both of us will sneak back into pants as often as possible."

Quenton could restrain himself no longer. "But where is the Dragon's Stone?"

Jack chuckled and pointed. "Under the throne. Cadell's sitting on it." Jack moved toward the throne. "Hey, Miranda? Would you like to appoint me as liaison to the dragons, since I'm bonded to the Dragon's Stone? That way, we can give it back to the dragons with honor." Jack waved his wand, and an oval gray river rock appeared, glowing, in his left hand. "By the way, it says DeAngelo is safely tied up and asleep in Tilda's room at the school. We'll get him later."

Miranda nodded, her grin crafty. "What will we do with our sire?"

"Oh, let him watch you rule. You see, he gets what he wants, just not the way he wants. Neither you nor I were raised on the concept of one gender being better than another." Jack shrugged.

They all nodded. Only humans and dragons of Honalee ranked the female above the male.

"That I can agree with." Miranda's voice remained cautious. "I do intend to insert equality slowly, over time. 'Tis only fair, but the people will accept a change such as this only over the course of a lifetime."

"I've got no problems with that." Jack shrugged and turned to Cadell. "There's a saying in the world where I grew up. 'Do not meddle in the affairs of dragons, for you are crunchy and taste good with ketchup'."

"What's ketchup?" they all chorused.

Jack sighed. "You guys sure know how to ruin a good joke."

Lena Austin

Lena Austin has lived a long and adventurous life. Now she enjoys telling tales and sprinkling them with memories of her adventures as a Dominatrix, 900-line girl, biker, and bad girl. Now in her 60s, she's not inclined to take up knitting, you know. Being a professional liar is so much more fun.

Lena at Changeling: changelingpress.com/lena-austin-a-11

Changeling Press E-Books

More Sci-Fi, Fantasy, Paranormal, and BDSM adventures available in e-book format for immediate download at ChangelingPress.com -- Werewolves, Vampires, Dragons, Shapeshifters and more -- Erotic Tales from the edge of your imagination.

What are E-Books?

E-books, or electronic books, are books designed to be read in digital format -- on your desktop or laptop computer, notebook, tablet, Smart Phone, or any electronic e-book reader.

Where can I get Changeling Press E-Books?

Changeling Press e-books are available at ChangelingPress.com, Amazon, Apple Books, Barnes & Noble, and Kobo.

ChangelingPress.com